Like A Tree
Without Roots

Like A Tree Without Roots

Teresa Ann Willis

Àṣẹ
PUBLISHING

New York

Cover design and photography:

Tewodross Melchishua
soulsuite.com

Model: Shannon Johnson

If you white, you all right
If you brown, stick around
If you black, get back baby, get back!

And if you believe that jack
Then you're a dope
And there is no hope
Because black is fine
And I thank God it's mine!

To the children of the African Diaspora!

Contents

Planted in strange soil
protect me with a fierce love
so that I can thrive

CHAPTER 1

I didn't know it would hurt so bad. I think it scared me more than it hurt, really. The first time. But this time I was mad. It seemed as though the whole right side of my head was throbbing, and I was cursing and crying at the same time.

"Shit!" I threw the hot comb into the sink and quickly placed my hand over my ear. With my left hand, I turned on the cold water to dampen the comb's fire, and I didn't care who heard the searing "sisssssssss" – or my outburst for that matter.

I can't believe I'm still doing this, I thought as I waved away steam. I was mad lucky the first time I tried to straighten my hair. No burns, at least not to my ear. I did take out a small section of hair and my scalp felt like it was on fire, but my mom didn't find out so as far as I was concerned, it hadn't been that bad. We'd had a half-day at school and my older brother was supposed to be watching me. He walked me home from school, made us both sandwiches then dared me to leave the apartment as he headed outside.

A few days earlier, I'd snuck into my mom's closet and climbed up to her top shelf in search of that little box. I'd seen the picture on the box a million times – in beauty salons where my mom got her hair done, in *Teen Scene* magazine, in the music videos and in my head. The woman on the box starred in the movie in my head that I played over and over and over – on my way to school, on the way home from school and when I looked in mirror. When I brushed my teeth, she smiled at me with her cocoa butter skin, high cheek bones, arched eyebrows, her slender White-girl nose and her hair – her hair, parted down the middle was long... silky... black. . . shiny.

But I couldn't understand the instructions so I put it back.

As soon as my brother shut the door that day, though, I ran and got the hot comb I'd spotted while I was looking for the little box. If I couldn't figure out how to give myself a perm, then I was going to do the next best thing. I'd been begging my mom for a perm. Begging her!

"You have a perm."

"Yes, and I'm grown."

I glared at her. Then I tried whining. "Yolanda's mother perms her hair. And Keyla has a perm."

"Um hum and by the time they're fourteen, all their hair is going to be gone. You'll be thanking me then."

They are fourteen and they still have hair I thought as my ear throbbed like the bass bouncing out of backseat car speakers. I screamed silently every time I replayed her words. Most of the girls I knew either had perms or braids. Some were even starting to get weaves. Maybe some of their hair *had* fallen out.

And?

You couldn't even tell it was fake hair sometimes until you were right in their faces. And, *thank you, mommy, for saving me? For saving my hair?* Not even close. Try, *Why I am cursed and how long is this going to last?*

I put my hand underneath the faucet to gather as much cold water as I could. I leaned my head over the sink and threw the water onto my ear which was now red and still throbbing. Soon, I'll have a nasty black scab, I thought. *As if you weren't already black enough*, the evil part of me said to the part that didn't want to hear it but had been hearing it for way too long.

When I raised my head and stared at my reflection, this time, *it* stared back. She wasn't smiling like she always did, and her skin wasn't cocoa butter or caramel or any shade that made boys light up and strain their necks to stare at you long after you'd passed them by because it wasn't her skin. She wasn't the lady on the relaxer kit and she wasn't the girl in the music video. She was me.

Black. Dirty. African.

I always thought it was stupid when kids called me an African since they knew I was African American born right here in Harlem. But all throughout elementary school, it was the same thing every day: "Oooohhh, you dirty, wipe that dirt off your face." Or, "Tar baby." Or, "She burnt." Or "Bead-a-bead." And when they were really trying to be hateful, "African booty scratcher!"

I grabbed a towel and dried my face. I always did wonder why Africans were so black. *Why am I so black?* Mama Roxie is black. Night-sky black. She lives in South Carolina and everyone says I look like her. I love my grandmother, but I don't want to look like her. I want to look like my mom, who's light skinned, and my brother who is too. But I look like my dad who looks like Mama Roxie.

I wish she were here now to stop my ear from hurting and to help me do something with this hair since it looks even worse than before. Usually, after I used the hot comb, I'd open the window so the smoke could escape, and I'd stick the hot comb outside and wave it in the air to make it cool faster. This time, I left it in the sink so my mom could see it. I'm in the eighth grade, 'bout to be in the ninth, I thought, and I'm old enough to get a perm. Or at least braids. Maybe if she saw the hot comb, she'd get a clue – a real clue this time.

When I was ten she did start letting me get a press and curl, but that only lasts a week and not even then if it gets wet. All my friends kept asking me why I didn't have a perm and when I finally got the press and curl everyone thought I had a perm.

"Oooohhh, Jasmine, you got a perm." Dionna was so happy for me, like I her was her daughter. "Don't you feel good now?" She asked me. I did feel good until a week later when they all started saying, "Oooohhh Jasmine, your naps are sticking up," and I would say, "Oh, I got caught in the shower or I got caught in the rain I'll fix it tonight." I couldn't fix it then, and I don't have time to do anything now, since, if I don't leave right away, I'm going to be late for school.

I smoothed back my hair, put a black scrunchy around the fistful I'd gathered into a pony tail – which was more like a rabbit's tail, really – and I threw on my Old Navy hoodie even though it was almost summer and starting to get hot in New York City. I left my apartment wearing my blue Converse kicks, a pair of jeans and my burgundy hoodie, and I intended to keep my hoodie on as long as I could, no matter how hot it got.

I shoved open the lobby doors to my building and was immediately blinded by the morning sun. I hated walking to school. And I hated riding the subway. But there was no use fantasizing about my mom having a car since there was no way she would drive me even if she did because school was only twenty blocks away.

Ebonee and I walked to elementary school together but all that involved really was a walk through the playground since the school was next door to our projects. If we hadn't moved, she and I would ride the train together.

Sometimes I wished we hadn't moved. Our apartment was nicer now, but we knew our neighbors more when we lived in Mears. Everybody was always hanging out. Talking. Getting loud. Little kids would be running around on the playground, playing one minute, getting mad at each other the next and just as quickly being friends again like nothing ever happened.

Now it seemed like all we did was live in our apartment. There were benches to sit on inside the iron gate that surrounded our building, but the only people who sat out there were old people. And when kids did try to play in there, they were yelled at before they even got started.

"Don't throw that ball around my flowers!" Did you plant the flowers, I wondered. How were they her flowers? I thought flowers came from God. I didn't know God was an old wrinkled lady with glasses. "And? What *would* happen if a ball accidentally hit the flowers?"

That's what I wanted to say to the grandma who said that to that little kid last week. Then when she looked at me cross-eyed like who was I to say something to her in the first place, I was going to say, "Yeah! That's what I thought," then walk away. Let me stop lying. I'd be running so fast. And I'd have to hide every time I saw her since if she ever figured out my apartment number and told my mom, I'd be dead.

I got on the subway at 116th Street and exited at Lenox and 135th. I walked past the hospital and past the Schomburg where my cousin, Imani, went every Saturday for the Junior

Scholars program. Whenever I was outside, I tried to block out everyone and everything and get to where I was going as fast as I could, so instead of seeing the people gathered in front of the Schomburg, I saw Imani and the other Junior Scholars at their yearly Youth Summit, dancing and acting and spitting poems about what it was like being a teen growing up in America.

They'd had their graduation last month, and they showed a video collage of all the projects they worked on during the year. I smiled when I saw my cousin looking too cute with her braids and her Aeropostale hoodie interviewing people on the street about losing their jobs or not even having a job in the first place. She interviewed one woman who said food was getting so expensive she had to stop buying cereal. Even though we were in the same grade, Imani was a year younger than me, but she was holding it down like a professional out there.

As soon as I turned the corner, I heard Amber and Dionna, even before I saw them, since they were laughing and getting loud like they always did. I watched as they stopped to talk to a man standing near the stop sign. He had long locs and a black linen afghan that hung down to his knees almost. As I walked closer, I could tell he was saying something serious. He was still talking when Dionna cut him off and said in a sing-song voice, "Oh, okay, we will." She and Amber turned and walked away but he kept talking.

They laughed, threw back their heads then waved hello.

"Heeeyyyy Jazz."

"Heeeyyyy!"

As she reached the front steps, Dionna unbuckled her belt and pulled it from around her waist. Several kids had begun the practice of starting their strip tease early so everybody could get through the metal detectors quicker. She was wearing Baby Phat jeans and a powder puff blue, crew neck Hollister T-shirt with the words *Hollister 1922* emblazoned on the front.

"What was that man talking about?" I asked Amber and Dionna as I joined them in the strip search line.

"He asked if we knew what happened in 1922."

"Is he crazy?"

"I said, I know the company that makes Hollister was started in 1922, and he shook his head and said 'young sister, nooooo.'" Dionna began imitating him – shaking her head and lowering her voice. "Young sister, noooo."

We burst into laughter.

"Then he started talking about Marcus Garvey and how in 1922 the FBI finally indicted him and closed down his business 'cause he was trying to organize Black people."

"He meant Marcus Garvey Park, right?" Amber asked.

"You are so ignorant."

"No, wait" Amber said and shook her head. "Who is Marcus Garvey again?"

Dionna laughed then went about schooling Amber. "Marcus Garvey, the Black leader who wanted everyone to go back to Africa or something," she said and waved her hand as if it were too much of a nuisance to be one hundred percent accurate."

Amber looked puzzled. "Wasn't he from Jamaica?"

"So, why don't he come in here and be our teacher?" I wanted to know. All three of us turned and looked in his direction. "Hey," I yelled. "You wanna come teach us? Come in here and teach us."

"They don't want me in there," he yelled back. "I'm too dangerous."

"Oh shit, he crazy," I said and pushed Dionna forward.

* * *

The bell rang letting us know it was time for lunch. I gathered up my backpack and bolted for the door. As soon as I entered the hallway, I spotted the Assistant Principal. She didn't waste any time yelling at me. "Take off that hoodie," she barked. "Next time, I'll confiscate it." She always had to talk to us with an attitude – like she was on her period every day.

I rushed to the bathroom to see what I could do with my hair now that it was on display. I locked eyes with the face in the mirror and forced a fake smile her way. I sighed, leaned in closer, cocked my head slightly and used my middle finger to push up my right eyebrow. I cocked my head slightly in the opposite direction and did the same thing with my left eyebrow.

Ebonee said she'd arch my eyebrows for me and that today we'd buy makeup and an eyebrow arch. She said it was actually good they were so thick since I wanted them tapered like Halle Berry. But still, she told me, if I really wanted them to look like Halle's, I'd have to go to a professional.

Halle's face stared at me in the mirror and I smiled. My Hershey Bar, dark chocolate skin had morphed into syrupy-sweet glazed caramel skin. The kind of see-through caramel that coats popcorn and browns it until it's just right. It was the same skin color as the woman on the relaxer kit. The same skin color as the women you see on the magazines.

"Craaaaaaccckkkk!"

My body jerked sideways and my hand instinctively grabbed at my chest. "Girl, you scared me!"

"Sorry," Dionna said as we both laughed. The bathroom door was broken and if you pushed it open with too much force, it slammed against the wall and sounded like the first pop of a firecracker. "What happened to your ear?"

"Did you bring your flat iron with you?"

"You burned yourself?"

"Yes."

"I have it, but I can't do it now," she said as she reached over and tried to smooth back my naps.

"Can't you just touch it up?"

"I have to meet with Ms. Ringwuld. She's trying to get me into this business high school so when I open my hair salon, I'll know what I'm doing and people won't take advantage of me. I can do it after school." This time she reached over and tried to smooth out my side edges. "I told you to just let me put a relaxer in it."

I glared at her with my I'm-gonna-kill-you-if-you-say-that-again stare. Really it was my mom I wanted to kill.

"Your mom's crazy," Dionna said and shook her head in protest. "How she gonna have a perm and you can't get one? That don't make no sense."

It didn't make any sense. Neither did my hair. I took one last hopeless glance in the mirror before heading to the cafeteria. Halle was gone. Jasmine was still there. My hair didn't look any different than it usually did, really. All I could do was run my hands over it one last time to smooth it down.

I entered the hallway just in time to see JaVon sneak behind Derrion, yank off his baseball cap and take off running. JaVon brushed by me, almost knocking me over, then he zig-zagged and 'my badded' his way through rush hour at MLK Middle School.

"Why you running? Why you running?" Derrion half laughed as he shouted at JaVon.

"Stoooopppp," Shayla yelled as Jason grabbed her from behind and struggled to put her in a head lock. "I said stop!" She was screaming and giggling in the same breath. Down the hall, another boy was manhandling another girl who was also trying to wrestle herself out of his grip and raising her voice in protest.

It was our usual hallway ritual where, if you weren't being accidentally bumped in to, you were being playfully slapped on the head, if you were a boy, or bear hugged, manhandled or felt up, whether you liked it or not, if you were a girl. If you were a teacher, forget it. All they did was yell and scream and try to squeeze their way through just like the students.

No one even thought about getting an attitude if someone bumped into them because it happened all the time. Unless someone was having a bad day or in a bad mood. Then, if they didn't feel like getting bumped or pushed, they'd say "excuse me" with enough attitude so you knew it was best to just move out of their way. But mostly, we just bumped into each other, not noticing half the time and not really caring when we did notice. In New York, it was crowded everywhere you went so you just got used to it.

I reached the cafeteria to find the usual crowd clumped into their familiar groups as they waited for the line to die down. I walked past Jocelyn and Lenelle and a few other Haitian girls who smiled and said hi. A few feet away, some Jamaican girls sounded as though they were arguing. They weren't. Just loud as hell I thought and shook my head. Then I spotted Ebonee talking to Trayvon and Kyesha, but why was Ylenny there?

I can't stand Puerto Rican girls. You think you all that. Just because you can go out with Puerto Rican boys, Dominican boys and African American boys you think you mad cool. You ain't no better than us, really. Living in the same projects and getting pregnant at a fifteen, just like us. Twelve really.

"Hey Jazz," Ebonee said and kissed me on the cheek.

Trayvon leaned his right shoulder into my left shoulder, giving me his version of a hug.

"Hey Jazz." Ylenny smiled and waited for me to speak.

I cut my eyes at her then turned to Ebonee. Ylenny needed to understand that she was not, in fact, all that, and I didn't appreciate her hanging with my BFF.

"Jazz?" Ebonee looked at me like I was crazy.

I whispered, but not low enough to keep Ylenny from hearing, "Let's just go. You know she was talking about you yesterday." Ylenny was dumbfounded. I'd pulled a lie out of my mouth the way a magician pulls flowers out of his closed-tight fist. It had come from nowhere and she wasn't having it.

"You Black bitch."

Black! The word 'Black!' knocked me upside the head. It kicked me in the stomach too and my insides began to pulsate with pain. I felt sick. The kind of sick you feel when you find out the whole school knows your secret — the one secret no one, not even God, is ever supposed to know. Ylenny hadn't called me a bitch, she called me a 'Black bitch.'

"You racist, that's so racist," two onlookers said, visibly disgusted with Ylenny. That struck me as strange since one of those very same girls had spent half the third grade calling me black!

I looked over at Ebonee. Her mouth was hanging open. She couldn't believe what Ylenny had just said. Even though I'd lied, it didn't matter now. Ebonee would never speak to Ylenny again. Knowing that gave me the courage to say some of the words that had been living inside me.

"You think you all that 'cause you Puerto Rican." I was in her face now knowing for sure Ebonee had my back.

"So hateful sometimes." I turned around and saw that Jocelyn and her ugly ass had walked up.

"Mind ya business, you African booty scratcher."

"I'm not African, I'm Haitian, you black cockroach."

"You just as black as I am."

"Ohhhhh!" A seventh-grader covered her mouth with her hand, not believing what she'd just heard.

"Y'all racist," someone else said.

"Jazz stop!" Ebonee pulled me by the arm.

I yanked away from her and ran through the lunchroom. I knew if I didn't get out of there right away, I'd unleash all the evil thoughts I'd ever had. Then maybe the evil part of me would be gone and never haunt me again. But if I did that the whole school would hate me; try to kill me really.

I kept running until I hit the double doors. As soon as the door swung open, I erupted like a volcano releasing its lava flow. My chest heaved as I struggled to muffle my crying. When that didn't work, I quickened my steps. I didn't want anybody to see me and I didn't want to see anybody. For a quick second, I closed my eyes thinking that would quiet my tears.

"Upppph! Jasmine, slow down." I'd bumped into Ms. Ervin. She grabbed hold of my shoulders and stared down at me. "What happened," she asked the same way my mom did when I used to run to her crying. I tore away from her and ran into the girl's bathroom.

"Jasmine!"

Ms. Ervin ran after me, and I heard her come in.

"Jasmine?" She waited for me to respond. "Jasmine!" This time she insisted on a response.

"Yes?"

"Are you feeling safe right now?"

"Yes."

"Okay. You're not in any danger?"

"No."

"Okay."

I could hear her exhale. She walked closer to the bathroom stall I was hiding out in. "Do we need to call your mother?"

"Call her for what." My words were laced with venom. Had I been a snake they would have punctured the bathroom door, penetrated Ms. Ervin's skin and killed her on the spot. Why would you call her, I thought. This is all her fault.

"You're really upset." Ms. Ervin didn't speak for what seemed like a long while. "But you're not in any danger, so that's good." She paused again like it was my turn to speak.

"Jasmine, I need to know what's going on or I will call your mother."

"I'm having a bad day."

"What's going on?"

Ms. Ervin waited patiently for me to answer as I continued crying silent tears.

"Jasmine, what happened?" She can't stay in here forever, I thought. "Jasmine, I have to meet with a student now, but I want you to come by after school – no wait, I can't meet today. Tomorrow morning. Can you get here early and meet with me? I have something I want to share with you."

"What?"

"Something I think you'll relate to. A poem."

I heard Ms. Ervin leave. I didn't know if I'd get up early to meet with her or not, but I told her I would. I did like poetry. I wrote poetry sometimes but more often, I wrote stories. From the time I was six, I wrote short stories.

Stories about people nobody else cared about. In my stories, the protagonist was usually a girl. She might start out shy but then she'd grow into the girl who was everybody's best friend. In my other stories, I'd write about a girl who could go anywhere she wanted and do anything and say anything she felt like saying to anybody.

When I was ten, I wrote a story about a girl at the prom who looked just like the lady on the relaxer kit. Of course, she got all the attention from the boys and the girls. Then there was this other girl who just stood in the corner, eating all the cake because nobody asked her to dance. The whole night, all she did was eat cake and watch everyone else dance. The girl eating the cake felt bad and decided she should share some cake with the girl who looked like the lady on the relaxer kit.

So, she cut her a nice piece of cake and got a fork and a napkin and gave it to her. What the girl didn't know was that she had put a spell on the cake and the next day, all her hair fell out. I told my mom the story was for English class and she had to read it to see if I'd spelled everything right and if it made sense. She liked it and she said I was a good writer. She asked me if I'd thought about writing books or becoming a screen writer. She didn't get it at all.

When I came home from my fifth-grade prom, I told my mom how happy I was and that I had a good time. I looked beautiful, like Cinderella with the puffy dress. Or so I thought! All the other girls were wearing short dresses, everybody except me and Ebonee. But I was the ugly little freak that nobody wanted to dance with. I just stood at the table eating cake all night.

I would do anything for a piece of cake right now. My stomach was growling, and going back to the cafeteria was out. There were two periods left in school and all I wanted to do was go home and get in bed and go to sleep. For a long, long time.

Ebonee and I have dance class after school today, I thought. In dance class, the evil part of me seemed to take a break because all I thought about, really, was how good it felt to be dancing and moving my body to the hip hop beats bouncing out the boom box in the community center. But what was I going to say to Ebonee about why I'd lied about Ylenny? Maybe I'll skip dance class. Maybe I'll text Dionna and let her put a relaxer in my hair.

CHAPTER 2

I slept through sixth period, and in seventh period, instead of going to Ms. Deveraux's class to turn in my lab like I'd said, I left school early since I didn't want to run into Ylenny. I couldn't face Ebonee either so I headed for the library. There I could sit down and read *Teen Scene* magazine instead of standing up and reading it at the store. I'd spent a lot of afternoons there, when dance class was over, doing my homework and sometimes everybody else's too.

I looked at the clock on the wall. I had turned off my Sidekick after lunch since I knew Ebonee would be texting me. I'd been here for an hour almost. They're probably just finishing their warm ups, I thought. Dance class was the one place where I wasn't a skinny little freak. Nobody cared how I looked or whether my hair was permed. All they cared about is whether or not you could dance. I couldn't believe I was hiding out at the library waiting for my mom to get home instead of dancing with Ebonee and the rest of our class.

When I looked at the clock again, it was almost six. I gathered up my back pack, returned the magazines I'd been reading and headed home. Fifteen minutes later, I opened the front door of our fifth-floor apartment, dropped my backpack on the living room sofa and went into the kitchen. Instead of my mom, my Aunt Angie was standing there sending a text message on her Blackberry.

"What are you doing here?"

"And how are you?"

"Where's mom?" I was insistent this time. I didn't mean to be rude to my favorite aunt, but this was a life-and-death matter.

"She had an emergency at work. She'll be home soon." She paused and looked at me.

"What's wrong?"

"Nothing."

"You don't look like nothing's wrong." She waited for me to respond. "You don't *sound* like nothing's wrong." She paused again. "You wanna talk about it" she asked softly.

"I need to talk to mom!"

My nastiness caught Aunt Angie off guard. The last time I asked my mom for a perm, she called her over to tell me how beautiful my natural hair was. But if natural hair is so beautiful, I said, why does mom have a perm? Why doesn't she have locs like you? This time, I hadn't even talked to her and Aunt Angie was here already. She doesn't have an emergency, I thought. She's an evil, mind-reading witch who's out to torture her only daughter.

"She should be home in a couple of hours, but right now we've got to make dinner. You put on the water and I'll start chopping."

Aunt Angie offered me a fist pound. I left her hanging for a few seconds then half-heartedly tapped her fist. Even though she was the last person I wanted to see right now, making pasta primavera with her was one of my favorite things to do.

"So how was school?"

I filled the pot three-quarters full with water and pretended I didn't hear her.

"Let me try this again. Jasmine, how was school?"

Aunt Angie's tone signaled to me that I'd better stop acting stupid and answer her.

"It was fine," I lied.

"Do you have any homework?"

"Yes."

"Anything interesting?"

"Some Columbus and the Caribbean shit—" she cut her eyes toward me. "—I mean stuff."

"So you're studying slavery?"

"How'd you know? What does Columbus have to do with slavery?"

She looked at me as though my question surprised her.

"So, you know that on his second voyage, Columbus began enslaving the people in the Caribbean and he forcibly took five-hundred of them back to Spain, right?"

"I know he came to America in 1492 and that he killed a lot of Indians."

"So, he and some other Europeans actually landed in the Caribbean. Today we call where he landed the Bahamas."

"But that's not America."

"So," Aunt Angie began, "Columbus didn't discover America."

"I know. You can't discover something if there's already people there."

"Right, but what I'm telling you is that there was no America. There were islands in the Western hemisphere where people were fishing and hunting and farming. Making their own tools. Canoes. Then Columbus comes along and starts claiming and renaming the islands." Aunt Angie paused. "So what do you have to do for your homework?"

I retrieved the handout from my backpack and began reading out loud.

"After we read this, we have to— what? You will use pen and paper (not a computer) to complete this assignment. With your dominant hand (right hand if you're right-handed, left hand, if you're left-handed) ask Christopher Columbus this question, *'Was it worth it? For the little gold you got from the Tainos and all the money you got from the king and queen, was it worth killing and enslaving the Tainos whom you said were kind, peaceful people?'* And with our non-dominant hand, we have to answer that question."

"Let me see that." Aunt Angie took my handout and began to read. "This is excellent. So, when you write with your left hand, that will be Columbus's answer to your question."

"That's mad crazy."

"No, it's brilliant. You'll see."

Aunt Angie and I finished preparing the pasta and the salad and we sat down to eat. She asked what time Dalani would be here, and I told her he was working on his afterschool film project and that I thought he had to work tonight also. She wanted to know when the film would be finished, but that I couldn't answer. Dalani and I rarely talked to each other when we were both here at the same time. We used to talk, especially about sports, but ever since dad left, he just kept to himself.

"Can I ask you a question?"

"Sure."

"Why do we have to study slavery?"

"Let me ask you a question? Why you do have to study—" Aunt Angie took a second to formulate her answer, "—the Revolutionary War, or what happened in ancient Greece or Rome? Or why do you have to study the Holocaust?"

I just looked at her. She stared back, though her stare was far more compassionate than mine. "Because all those things are over. And people aren't still ODing about all that stuff."

"When you think about slavery, what images come up for you?

"What?"

"When you think about slavery, what do you see, when

you think about it?"

"Slaves."

"What else?"

"I don't want to talk about this."

"I know. I don't either, really. I'd rather talk about how far we've come and how the past has been made right, but that hasn't happened."

"You and Ms. Ervin are twins."

"Who's Ms. Ervin?"

"My Social Studies teacher."

"Why do you say that?"

"I asked her why we have to study slavery and she didn't answer my question either. She said I'd have to study slavery to find out why it's important to."

"Smart lady."

"What do you mean the past hasn't been made right?"

"Doesn't school end next week?"

"Yes."

"So maybe—"

"It's a mini-unit."

"—maybe you can come over this weekend and we can talk then. Once you've studied it a little more, then we can talk about the past and what hasn't been made right."

Lots of things haven't been made right, I thought as I finished my salad and looked over at my aunt.

"So, why did you loc your hair?"

"I love the way it looks."

"But why didn't you want to look like other women with straight hair?"

"I did. At one point."

"Why?"

"Why? That's a good question. Because, that's all I knew, I think. I wanted to look like what was popular, like everybody else, I guess."

"What happened to make you stop wanting to be like everybody else?"

"I grew up," she said and paused. "At some point, I started liking this style more than straight hair, and it became more important for me to feel comfortable about how I looked instead of wanting to look a certain way because it was what made people comfortable or what men liked."

Yeah right, I thought.

"On top of all that, it mattered to me to wear my hair natural and to stop putting harmful chemicals in it."

"I want long hair."

"Then wear it natural." I stared Aunt Angie down. The venom inside me was seeping out again. Victim number two, coming right up I thought. "The chemicals and all the heat makes hair break off so it's harder for it to grow."

"I want long, *straight* hair."

"Why?"

I didn't answer her.

Aunt Angie stared at me. She was making me uncomfortable. "Probably for the same reason I did," she said finally. "You know your mom's right for not letting you perm it."

"Will you do it for me? With a relaxer kit?"

"Jasmine—"

"Please? Then she'll see how good it looks and it won't damage my hair."

"I'll talk to your mom—"

"Yesssss! Thank you!"

"—I'll talk to your mom about our conversation. And when you come over—"

"When I come over, what?"

"Jasmine, your hair is short, but that doesn't make you any less beautiful. You have beautiful brown eyes that sparkle when you smile." Aunt Angie waited for me to look at her, then she offered me her smile. "You're a gifted writer." She paused again. "Jasmine, you're brilliant and you're beautiful."

No, you're beautiful, I thought. Just like mom. Even with her locs, Aunt Angie had beautiful bronzed skin – a few shades darker than mom, but still beautiful, like guys like. Beautiful like Ebonee. Not black, like me.

I used to pray for the day when I could get my skin bleached like Gavin. His mom started him on bleaching cream when he was five. Gavin wasn't really dark dark, and to me, he was so cute. I had a crush on him from the second grade until the fourth. Then, one day, after Science class, Jalissa and Jahira tried to start a fight with me when I sat next to Gavin, even though that wasn't my seat, and Ms. Rivera let me sit there anyway. Jalissa was jealous because she liked him too. A few days later, at recess, Gavin ran into me and knocked me down on the concrete. Hard.

"Jasmine, WHAT IS GOING ON?"

I was lost in a succession of painful memories – memories that darted in and out of me like the sun fading in and out of the clouds. Aunt Angie looked at me like I was lost somewhere and she wished she could find me. Sometimes, I couldn't even find me. I used to constantly daydream about how long it would take to get lighter if I started using bleaching cream and how long it would take Ebonee to notice; how long it would take Gavin to notice. Until that day he knocked me down on the playground. He claimed it was an accident, but we both knew it wasn't. From that day on, I wanted to kill him.

Aunt Angie pushed back her chair, stood up and softly cupped my shoulders. "Let's clean up then we'll both get started on our homework."

"You're gonna help me," I asked looking up at her.

"My homework, I'm doing my work, paper work. Your mom shouldn't be that much longer."

We put away the dishes and left the food on the counter for mom and Dalani. I went into the living room and grabbed my backpack. I walked past the picture of Mama Roxie sitting on the bookshelf and the picture of me, Dalani and mom hanging up in the hallway. I stopped in the bathroom to see if the hot comb was still there. It wasn't. Good, I thought. Maybe now she has a clue.

I opened the door to my room, threw my backpack on the floor and jumped onto my bed. As soon as I got started with the assignment, I had to put it down. I couldn't believe what I was reading. From the time he first saw the Tainos, Columbus was ODing on how he could get their gold and make them do whatever he wanted. He had made a deal with the King and Queen of Spain, and they paid him to go to India and find gold.

It was really crazy since, even though he was trying to get to India, he ended up in islands nobody knew existed— nobody except the people living there. He went there already knowing what he was going to do. That's messed up, I thought and shook my head. I opened my notebook and began writing.

> *Hey Christopher,*
>
> *Was it worth it? For the little gold you got from the Tainos and all the money you got from the King and Queen, was it worth killing and enslaving the Tainos who you said were kind and peaceful people?*

I put down my pen and reread the assignment: *Don't*

think. Just pick up the pen with your non-dominant hand and write. Don't erase anything. Write whatever comes out while you're holding the pen in your nondominant hand, and don't go back and edit what you've written.

>*Dear Jasmine,*
>
>*No. I think not. Even before I passed away, I knew this to be so. Mine was not a life well lived.*

That's it? Now what, I thought then decided to make up my own question.

>*So you introduced sugar cane to the people in the Caribbean and you made the Indians slaves. After you and your crew murdered them all, your son and others had African slaves. What made you think it was okay to force others to work so you could become rich? How is that fair?*
>
>*It's not. Greed. Arrogance. It's stupid. There are still many like me. Too many.*

Way too many. This shit is making me mad. I turned on my cell phone. Ebonee had sent me a text saying she was just now getting home and for me to call. I'd ignored her earlier texts. I didn't know how to talk to her about what happened in the cafeteria. Ebonee actually did have skin like Halle

Berry and hair that dangled down beyond her shoulders. We'd grown up together in Mears projects before me, my mom and Dalani moved out.

Even though we'd been friends for a long time, when we got to middle school, everything changed. We were still friends, but middle school was treacherous. It was hard being around her. She got all the attention and I got ignored or made fun of. But not like in elementary school when kids called you names to your face. Now they talked about you behind your back, but that was worse, really, since you never knew who you could trust.

"How'd it go?" Aunt Angie walked into my room to tell me that mom would be home in ten minutes.

I handed her my notebook. She read silently and nodded her head in affirmation.

"Call me tomorrow night and let me know how class goes. And Saturday we'll have a sleepover."

"And you'll do my hair?"

"I was thinking it would be fun if you, your mom and Imani came over. We can stay up, listen to music, talk."

"I thought it was going to be just you and me?"

"It'll be good for all of us to hang out."

"But you are going to talk to mom?"

"I already did and we both think a sleepover would be fun. I told her you were upset and wanted to talk."

"What'd she say?"

"Jasmine—" Aunt Angie paused, walked over to my bed and sat down. She put her arm around me. "—I know thirteen is a tough age, and I know your dad leaving has been difficult, but things aren't easy for her either. And on top of everything else, she's going through some craziness at work."

I shut down. I had no use for anything else that might come out her mouth. This ain't about her, I thought. It's about me! "Okay," I said and turned away. Out of the corner of my eye, I saw her smile. That was exactly what she wanted to hear. She gave me a hug and left my room. That was exactly what I wanted to see.

***

I woke up to the sound of my alarm beeping and a bird chirping outside my window. I didn't do my English homework. I didn't do the math puzzle Ms. Grant had given us for fun either. Columbus and his evildoers took up all the space in my brain, and I couldn't think straight after that. I didn't even talk to my mom other than to say, no, I was mad at something that happened in school . . . Ebonee and I had a fight but we're cool now. . . Yeah dance class was good. . . some girl lied and said I said something about Ebonee, but we talked and everything's cool.

I made stuff up and fed it to my mom all the time. She said the sleepover would be fun, and I could tell she wanted to say more, but for whatever reason, she didn't. She was exhausted from work so she ate dinner and went to bed. They're going to ambush me at the sleepover, I know it. I'll text Imani today and see what's up. I wish she went to MLK, but unfortunately, she lived in Brooklyn with my uncle and his wife.

I looked at the clock again and dreaded getting up and getting ready for school. What was Ebonee gonna say? And Ylenny? I at least had to do my English homework. I opened up my writing journal and thought for a minute. The bird outside my window kept chirping.

> *The sun wakes me up*
> *the birds belt out good morning*
> *as half the world sleeps*

I still had to do the math puzzle. And my hair. And Ebonee. It was way too much to think about, and I definitely didn't want to deal with Ebonee. Or Ylenny for that matter. I thought about all the lucky people on the other side of the world whose day was over.

> *The sun disappears*
> *crickets begin their night song*
> *half the world wakes up*

I'm in the wrong half. Maybe—

"Good morning!"

"Hi."

"Rise and shine, sleepy head."

"I'm up."

"So. You excited about our sleepover?"

Maybe I should tell her the truth, just this once. I nod my head and whisper yes.

"So, I have what I think is the greatest idea, and, oh I know how hard this is for you, but please tell me if you disagree. Just this once."

"You got jokes." I wasn't in the mood for her jokes, but right now, anything sounded better than the noise in my head.

"At our sleepover, let's all get makeovers."

"What kind of makeovers?"

"Whatever kind we want."

"Hair. Makeup. Clothes?—" I was starting to get excited, "—everything?" But a part of me was skeptical.

"So, clothes— maybe not clothes this time 'round. But everything else."

I didn't say anything for a long while. I couldn't bear asking my mom if that meant I could get a perm and having her say no. She broke the silence.

"What'd you write?"

"It's for English." I handed her my journal. "A haiku."

"The sun wakes me up birds belt out good morning as half the world sleeps. The sun disappears, crickets begin their

night song, half the world wakes up" She looked at me and
gently nodded her head. She motioned for me to move over,
and she snuggled up beside me. We're having the sleepover
now, I wanted to say. But in an instant, everything slowed
down, and I became fascinated watching my mom breathe.
Her stomach moved up, then back down. Then up again,
slowly. Then back down. I could see her thinking too.
Thinking about what she would say next.

"You've been really angry with me, for a while now."

Yup. I thought. Really, really angry.

"Jazz, you know it's just you, me and Dalani now. And
the older you both get, the more complicated things are."
She took a long breath in and pushed it out in a sigh. "I
know it's hard for you to believe this, but I am trying to
understand things from your perspective. And at the same
time, I'm having to deal with life out there in the world, you
know. And I know when I was working and going to school
at night, I know it wasn't good for you two."

"I missed you."

"I know."

She shifted. I watched her bring her hand to her eyes
and keep them there. "I'm here now, Jasmine." She wiped
her eyes then looked over at me. "I need to know what's
going on with you." It's amazing how fast your heart starts
beating when you want to tell someone how you're really
feeling, but you're afraid of how they might respond. "So,

we've both been giving each other space, actually more like the silent treatment, and I've let it go on way too long. I know why you're angry with your father, but why are you so angry with me?"

I just laid there staring at my Chris Brown poster.

"Do you even know or is this just something you've decided to do because, because you're thirteen-going-on-fourteen and one of your friends said this is what fourteen-year-olds do?"

My mom was so ignorant sometimes. Still, I didn't know if I was ready to speak the words that were up next in my head. "I wish I looked like you and Dalani." My mom snapped her head in my direction. She looked like I'd just told her I was pregnant.

"What do you mean? You mean you wish you were light-skinned?"

I nodded my head up and down.

My mom sighed a long, hard sigh like a tire with a nail stuck in it slowly releasing its last bit of air. Neither of us said anything for what seemed like ten minutes but really it was only a few seconds. *Nothing. That's what you say?* I didn't even try to hide my disappointment. I just shook my head and frowned. She turned toward the window.

"Do you hear that?"

"What?"

"The bird. She's singing to us."

"What?"

"She's singing Bob Marley. Listen." My mother closed her eyes and she started to sing that famous Bob Marley song telling you not to worry.

Oh, now you want to sing? I put as much venom into my next words as I could. "If it's singing Bob Marley, it's a he." She pretended she hadn't heard me and kept on singing. When I was younger, I was afraid of the dark, and my mom and dad used to sing me to sleep and kiss me goodnight. Then I felt like everything was going to be all right. And even though I didn't want it to, her happy song – Bob Marley's happy song – got inside me and made me want to sing along with her. It needed something else though. "Buh! Buh!" My beat box was right on time.

"Snap! Snap!"

Uh oh! Moms trying to keep the beat.

"One time!" my mom yelled, signaling for us to keep repeating the chorus. "Two times!"

It was my turn now. "Three ti-imz!," I said with more flavor than she even knew existed.

"Last time," she said as we ended our duet. For several seconds, we laid there, smiling. Then she looked over at me and whispered, "everything is gonna be all right," and, ever so softly, she kissed me. On the side of my face. In an instant, my throat felt like the Sahara Desert and my eyes threatened rain. But I didn't want to cry with her lying next to me so I fended off the storm.

"So, we'll talk about this. I'll be home late tonight," my mom paused, "—I have to deal with something at work. But tomorrow, we'll talk and fix dinner. Okay?" I closed my eyes and turned away from her. "Jazz?" Just go, I thought. She shifted and rolled herself out of the bed. I turned to see her standing there looking down at me. "It's ti-ime for school." She accompanied her words with a funky little head and shoulder move.

"Do I have to go? It's only a half-day."

She stared at me with raised eyebrows. "Text me and let me know how class goes."

My mom and I rarely talked when she came home. Staying out of each other's way had been a mutually agreed upon strategy. I guess she was changing her strategy. As soon as she left and closed the door, all my problems started screaming at me again like how dare I forget about them, even for a few minutes. I wished I could just avoid everybody. I couldn't face Ebonee, and I definitely needed to stay away from Ylenny. Thank God we only had a half day. With any luck I'd be able to avoid everybody.

CHAPTER 3

I knew I was going to see Ylenny on the train! And she was with Marisol, Tiara and Amarylis. Why did the popular girls always travel in a pack? Like a pack of dogs. Laughing and talking like they were the center of the universe. It's not like Ylenny really spoke to me before. So why was she trying to act like we were friends yesterday? And why was Ebonee hanging with her all of a sudden. Still, I wished I had never gotten in her face. If I could take back everything I said, I would. Not because it wasn't true. Not because I didn't really want to slap her Boricua face. But because I may have messed up bad with Ebonee.

As soon as the train doors closed, I reached for the handle of the door that connected one car to another. It was illegal to walk through the doors, supposedly because it was dangerous and you could die! I didn't know of anyone ever dying while walking between the cars, but I did know I had to get away from Ylenny.

I sat down even though I was getting off at the next stop. I flipped open my cell and was about to text Ebonee when I heard the subway doors open. I looked up and there they were, all four of them. Ylenny walked over and stood over me with her hand on her hip, and she stared down at me.

"So, what was that you said yesterday?" She paused and looked at me like I better answer her. "You lucky we on this train right now." She leaned in closer and lowered her voice.

"Bitch!"

The train prepared to stop as the words, "This is 135th Street" blared over the subway system speaker. I sat there, staring up at her with eyes that bulged with fear and begged for mercy. My heart beat faster and louder than it had a right to, and I prayed to God it didn't jump through my chest.

"You getting off?" I could feel the anger shooting out of Ylenny's pores like the heat that used to shoot out of our radiator at Mears, whether it was cold outside or not. There was no mercy to be had. That was clear. And I knew if I got off and there were no cops around, I was going to get a beat down.

"Oh, so that's your strategy."

Yup. That's my strategy.

"Stay on the train. We know where to find Your Black Ass."

I watched them walk down the stairs as the train carried me to the next stop. *We know where to find Your Black Ass! Your Black Ass! Your Black Ass!*

When I got off the train, I tried, unsuccessfully, to run past everybody walking up the steps. When I got outside, I immediately texted Ebonee. I didn't know if she'd been able to sneak her phone in or not. Since it was the end of the school year, most kids were sneaking them in instead of paying a dollar and leaving them at the corner store. What could they do, suspend us?

"Ylenny, Tiara, Marisol and Amarylis tryd 2 jmp me on the train"

I waited for Ebonee to text me back. After a couple of minutes when I still hadn't heard from her, I crossed the street, got on the train and headed back downtown. I got to school just before the late bell rang.

I checked my phone at least fifteen times during first period to see if Ebonee had texted me back. Maybe she didn't have her phone. Or maybe she couldn't care less if I got jumped. This was worse than fifth grade. Worse than getting knocked down by Gavin. I tried to not even think about Ebonee or Ylenny or what happened yesterday. I was supposed to be leading the discussion in Ms. Ervin's class, but I didn't want to think about that either.

Yesterday, after she handed back our final projects, she announced that we were going to do a mini-unit on slavery. Good, I remember thinking. *Maybe you can tell me why Africans are so black! And Haitians too. There are way too many Haitian kids in MLK—* Ms. Ervin had rudely interrupted my thoughts by asking us to write down everything we wanted to know about slavery. *It's not like we wanted to be slaves,* I wrote. *So why do we even have to discuss this?*

After she read our answers, she gave us another card and told us to write down what we thought life would be like for African Americans today if we hadn't had slavery. We weren't even supposed to be studying slavery. We'd spent all year covering U.S. History from Reconstruction to the present, and we'd already taken our eighth-grade Social Studies exam, so why were we going backward I wondered.

When we studied slavery last year, our teacher told us how slavery in New York wasn't as bad under the Dutch as it was under the British. We read parts of Uncle Tom's Cabin and we discussed Harriet Tubman and Frederick Douglass. We also memorized the names of slave and free states and discussed the Kansas-Nebraska Act and what that all meant. Now what, I wondered? What else is there to know except that Black people were treated worse than dogs by White people so now we have Black History month and Barack Obama might be the first Black president!

Nobody wanted to talk about this, especially at the end of the school year. Nobody except Sekou who wanted to know what things would be like today for White people if there hadn't been slavery?

* * *

It was time for Ms. Ervin's class and I hadn't heard anything from Ebonee. I looked for her after first period, but when I couldn't find her and didn't hear from her I assumed she hated me. *I messed up. Bad. I don't even want to go to Social Studies.*

"So, before we talk about the readings," Ms. Ervin began, "let's do one last circle exercise."

Oh god. We had to get up and stand in a circle. Ms. Ervin was going to read some statements, and if we agreed with what she said, we would step into the circle. If we didn't, we'd stay put.

"So, let's begin our exploration of United States chattel slavery by understanding our own power as teachers and learners," Ms. Ervin said as she walked to the corner of the room. We crowded together, like we'd done several times before, and formed a circle around the perimeter of our classroom. There were twenty-seven of us and not much space. She wasted no time getting started.

"Africans are disgusting."

Several kids step forward. Ms. Ervin nodded and they stepped back, awaiting the next statement.

"Africans are a strong people."

About half the group stepped forward while the other half didn't.

"African-Americans are lazy and don't work."

Five students stepped forward. JaVon looked at them and shook his head. Amber's eyes grew big as she stared them down.

"Whaaat?" Dionna half whispered.

"Excuse me!" That's all Ms. Ervin had to say. During this exercise, there was no passing judgment and absolutely no snide remarks or commenting on someone's decision to step up or stay back. We weren't even supposed to use any body language, really. Ms. Ervin continued with her statements.

"African-Americans are a strong people."

Everybody moved forward.

"Jamaicans outlawed slavery in 1834."

What? Jamaicans didn't have slavery, I thought. Nobody moved. How could we? We didn't agree or disagree with what she'd said, we just didn't know what she was talking about!

"The United States outlawed slavery in 1865."

Everybody moved forward.

"Puerto Ricans outlawed slavery in 1873.

What? I wondered again. At the last second, JaVon stepped into the circle, knowing he didn't know anything about slavery in Puerto Rico. But I guess he figured he had a fifty-fifty chance of being right. A few of us snickered and cut our eyes at him, even though we weren't supposed to.

"Cubans outlawed slavery in 1886."

Nobody moved.

"Brazilians outlawed slavery in 1888."

How long is this going to go on, I thought. Maybe if we had someone from Brazil here, they could step forward, if it's true.

"Last three," Ms. Ervin announced. 'Latinos are smart." Many kids moved quickly and stood proud when they entered the circle. I don't know why I didn't step forward right away, but it didn't matter. I tried to move forward nonchalantly as if it was no big deal. Of course Latinos are as smart as everyone else. Two kids, Tristan and Destiny never moved. Ms. Ervin nodded her head and we all stepped back.

"African Americans are smart."

It seemed as if we all moved forward together, in one fluid motion except that we didn't all move. I couldn't believe it. Several kids stayed back – Puerto Rican, Dominican. What the f___?

Last statement. I am smart. I am intelligent."

Everybody stepped forward. Ms. Ervin made it a point to look at each one of us and smile. "Okay, that's it," she said and we all went back to our seats. *What? She didn't do Jamaicans and Haitians. Why not?* I wanted to raise my hand and ask, but I didn't. *I can't believe those Spanish bitches just stood there. And Alfredo and Richard too!*

"We're going to work our way backward," she began. "So, Brazil did indeed outlaw slavery in 1888, the last South American country to do so. Cuba made slavery illegal in 1880 and every year in Puerto Rico on March 22, they celebrate Puerto Rico's abolition of slavery."

"When did Puerto Rico have slavery?" Kaitlyn asked.

"So Jasmine's going to lead the discussion on how this all got started. You can you start by telling us why the population of Borinquen, today known as Puerto Rico, went from

30,000 people in 1508 to less than 4,000 people six years later?"

"Greed, really. And murder."

"Tell us more."

"Christopher Columbus's son, Diego and Ponce de Leon and other *explorers* from Spain came to the island looking for gold. They made the Borinquen slaves and they started fighting."

Ms. Ervin interjected. "They *enslaved* the Borinquen?"

"They enslaved the Borinquen and then they killed the ones who starting fighting back and some killed themselves instead of becoming slaves—"

"Instead of becoming enslaved."

"—becoming enslaved. And diseases caused others to die."

"Excellent."

JaVon raised his hand. "Others ran away into the mountains."

"Yes," Ms. Ervin replied. "They were called Maroons. We'll read more about them tonight, Maroons in Cuba, Brazil, Jamaica and Florida, too."

"Florida?" There are mountains in Florida?"

"No, but there were many enslaved Africans who ran away to Florida. I realize that you're often taught about 'runaway slaves' as they're erroneously called, escaping north to freedom, but liberated Africans in the Carolinas and

Georgia escaped to Florida and lived among the indigenous people, the people already living there, write this down—" Ms. Ervin wrote the word indigenous on the white board.

"—So slavery wasn't something that happened only in North America. And once the indigenous in the Caribbean were wiped out, the Portuguese and later the British and the Dutch began trading goods for Africans. They took them to Puerto Rico, Jamaica, Cuba, Brazil and other Latin American countries, then to the U.S. And Mexico also."

Tiara raised her hand. "So you're saying that slaves from Africa were taken to Puerto Rico?"

Ms. Ervin shook her head no. Then, she went to her desk and got several eight-and-a-half-by-eleven inch laminated pictures. She held up pictures of dark-skinned African people, and they were all working. There was a farmer working on his farm (she said he was a rice farmer), an iron worker, a woman preparing food, another woman carrying water in a pot on her head, a goldsmith, a dressmaker, and someone sitting in the middle of a circle engaged with a group of people – a jeli she called him.

"So, the men, women and children who were kidnapped and put on ships and transported first to the Caribbean and to South America were, rice farmers, they prepared meals for their families, they made gold ornaments, they built buildings, they were dressmakers, story tellers, and mothers and fathers and ten-year-old sons and daughters."

Ms. Ervin stopped and waited for us to respond.

"The majority of the Africans transported were young men and young women. Their ages ranged from fifteen to thirty-five—

"Word?" Joseph asked. "I thought it was older people."

"That's OD." Derek didn't usually speak up in class.

"—Fifteen to thirty-five," Ms. Ervin continued, "but the men seeking to make the highest profit preferred to buy African people in their twenties." Ms. Ervin paused again. "Why weren't elders, or even Africans in their late thirties or in their forties desirable? Why didn't the business traders want them?" She asked.

"Because they were older."

"And? What about them being older didn't make good business sense?"

"JaVon raised his hand. "I guess 'cause they couldn't work as hard, maybe."

"Okay, what else?"

"Maybe they were sick, I don't know. I know people didn't live as long back then."

"Maybe, maybe not, but you're using good deductive reasoning, Keyla. So, the businessmen who traded goods for humans absolutely did look to capture the healthiest boys, girls, women and men. Younger people could work for long-er periods assuming nothing happened to them. In fact, the human traffickers specifically looked for those people who'd already had smallpox. Why?"

"Because they wouldn't get it again."

"Exactly."

"So, Ms. Ervin, you said traded goods for slaves. What did they trade," Alexis asked.

"I said traded goods for humans. For Africans."

"What's the difference?"

"So, you saw the pictures I just held up?"

"Yes."

"Someone talk about the differences between referring to these people as slaves versus referring to them as Africans. Jasmine."

Why you calling on me, I didn't raise my hand? "Well, I guess if the slaves, I mean Africans, were farming, raising their families and working just like we do today, then they weren't slaves until they got over here."

"So are you saying, then," JaVon began, "that when they got here they stopped being human beings?"

"What do you think?"

"I mean, they *were* slaves once they got over here and had to work in the fields. It's not like they could just leave." He paused for a second. "So yeah, they were slaves."

"But JaVon, your question was, did they cease being human beings?"

For a few seconds, it seemed like I just stopped thinking. I began slowly looking around the room, and as I did, my thoughts returned. I wished I could hear what everyone else was thinking. My own thoughts grew so loud that I was convinced everyone could hear me: *White people said we weren't human beings... they called us apes... they said we came from apes... that we were an inferior race... they treated us like dogs... worse than dogs...*

"No."

"No—" Ms. Ervin slowly moved her head from side to side "—They didn't stop being human beings," she said repeating JaVon's answer. "So, let's talk about the first couple of statements I read off. Africans are disgusting."

No one said a word.

"Several of you agreed with that statement."

Keyla raised her hand.

"I stepped in the circle. But I'm not talking about the Africans in this school, just in general."

JaVon stared Keyla down. He'd heard her say she would never be friends with any of the Africans in this school. We all had.

"Go on." Ms. Ervin wanted to hear more. So did I.

"What do you want me to say?"

"You said, 'in general.' What do you mean? How is it that Africans 'in general' are disgusting?"

"I don't know. I guess because they come from Africa."

"And why is that disgusting?"

"I don't know. Because it's Africa, I guess. That's where slavery started, or not started, but it's where slaves came from. It's just disgusting."

"She just said they weren't slaves," I said.

"But hasn't there always been slavery?" JaVon asked. "We learned in sixth grade that there were slaves back then.

"Back when?"

"In ancient Greece and Rome."

"Yes, there's always been slavery. Even in Ancient Africa. In Egypt for example and other countries in Africa."

"Whaaaat?"

"And even later in Africa, but we're not talking about slavery as it existed in the Americas. Those people were enslaved, yes, but their status was much different than what we refer to when we speak about slavery in America."

JaVon raised his hand. "How was it different?"

"Well, they could marry and own property, and, in some cases, become an heir to their master. In the Ashanti society for instance, it was common for an enslaved person to be adopted into the family. I'm not saying they weren't wrenched away from their own families and enslaved. I am saying they weren't viewed as property and they weren't treated like they were here and in Caribbean countries.

Ms. Ervin looked around the room. "So let's hear from others about what we've gone over so far. Tiana, you've been really quiet."

"Yeaaahhh because all this is blowing my mind. They never told us this before. And now you tellin' us this— it makes me think about things differently."

"What's different for you now?"

"It's like you said, they were human beings even though we always call them slaves. Like they were animals or something—"

"But they were treated like animals," Derek said as he shrugged his shoulders.

"—and I didn't know there were slaves in Puerto Rico. I know that in my family, we always looked down on the people who were darker, and I have this uncle who used to always say we came from Africa and everybody said he was crazy."

CHAPTER 4

I headed to my locker lost in thought about everything that had happened in Ms. Ervin's class. Everybody else was rushing to leave since we had all afternoon to do whatever we wanted. When I closed my locker, Ebonee was staring me in the face. Her first words were sarcastic.

"Thanks for texting me back yesterday."

"Did you get *my* text?"

"When?"

"This morning."

"My mom has my phone. So why didn't you text me back?"

"Sorry," I said. "But that shit was messed up."

"Jazz, what you said was messed up."

What? That's what you say to me, that what I said was messed up. Ylenny called me a Black bitch, I thought. I couldn't believe Ebonee didn't have my back. "What about what she said?"

"You know I'm half Puerto Rican.

"I wasn't talking about you, Ebonee! I wasn't talking about you!"

"Yeah, you were!"

I couldn't believe it. I never thought of Ebonee as Puerto Rican. Her mom and stepfather were African American, and she didn't speak Spanish. Her father had been killed a long time ago, in August of 1994, a few months before she was born and the same month I was born. I'd read about his murder online a couple of years ago. Manuel Alberto Torres was an undercover subway cop killed by a White off-duty cop who mistook him for a criminal when really, Mr. Torres had just gotten someone on the train, the real criminal, to drop his gun.

"And what was she supposed to have said about me anyway?" An earthquake invaded my stomach and I couldn't move. I couldn't think straight either. I was paralyzed. "You. were lying?"

I couldn't lose Ebonee. Even if I was jealous of her sometimes, we were like sisters. When her father died, my dad treated her like his daughter, like we *were* sisters. He and Mr. Torres had gone to high school together, and he looked out for Ebonee and both he and my mom were there for Ebonee's mom after the murder. The reason I was friends with Dionna and Amber is because they were friends with Ebonee.

"What the—

"Oh. My bad."

Anthony had bumped into me and pushed me up against my locker.

"Whatchu doing," Ebonee yelled and threw up her hands in disbelief. Anthony reached out and tried to hug Ebonee. She pushed him away.

"Mynigga, apologize!"

"I said my bad." Anthony didn't take his eyes off Ebonee.

"Can't you see she's upset!"

"Calm down. She still breathing. You know I love you, right? Right? And you know I'm your agent right. Right?" He leaned over and tried to kiss Ebonee. Again, she pushed him away. Ever since sixth grade, Anthony was one of a million boys who wanted to get with Ebonee. One day last year, he came up with the brilliant idea that if anyone ever asked her to model or act or be in a music video that she'd hire him as her business manager. That way he'd have a better chance of getting with her, in his mind at least, and he'd get rich at the same time.

"Nigga, get out of here. Can't you see we're discussing something!"

"Oh. My bad," he said and took off down the hall. "But you got my number," he shouted as he moved farther away. Text me. Today. Tonight. Tomorrow's okay too!"

"I can't stand this school," I said and looked over at Ebonee.

"What is wrong with you?"

"I just told you!"

"We have four days left and all of sudden you can't stand nobody? Were you mad because I was hanging out with Ylenny?" She waited for me to answer. "Okay, she's racist, I get that now, but what did she do for you to lie on her?"

"They tried to jump me on the train."

"Who?"

"Ylenny, Tiara, Marisol and Amarylis.

"When?"

"This morning. I tried to text you. They're probably waiting for me right now."

"Text Dionna and tell her and Amber to wait for us at the front of the school."

I quickly sent Dionna a text, and Ebonee and I made our way through the now empty hallway. I had never been in a fight. I had seen girls and boys get jumped before, but I never thought anyone would try to jump me. I weighed all of one-hundred pounds and the only thing I had going for me when it came to fighting was that I could run fast as hell.

"Hey, what's up?" Dionna asked us the second we walked outside.

"Ylenny tried to jump her this morning on the train."

"Why didn't you say something in Ms. Ervin's class?"

"Ylenny, Tiara Marisol *and* Amarylis," Ebonee said then asked if they'd seen any of them.

"Marisol and Amarylis left a few minutes ago, but I haven't seen Ylenny," Dionna offered. "Or Tiara."

"Okay, let's just start walking. But watch your back. Matter of fact, you and Amber walk ahead of us and when you turn the corner, let us know if you see any of them. If you do, one of you just turn around and walk back to us, and one of you just keep walking.

We made it onto Lenox Avenue without any sign of Ylenny and her crew.

"They all live in Mears, right?" Amber asked.

"Hell yeah," Dionna said.

"Tiara doesn't," Ebonee said.

"She moved?"

"Yeah. Why'd you say it like that?" Ebonee asked.

"Like what?"

"Hell yeah!"

"Cause, like Jazz said, a lot of Spanish girls do think they all that. And be owning projects just like we do!"

"You're stereotyping."

"No I'm not. And you know when they start talking Spanish around you, they be talking about you. My mom told us that a long time ago." Ebonee just shook her head like it was no use trying to convince Dionna she was wrong. "I'm not saying everybody, but there's so many haters in the world!" Dionna shook her head and frowned. "You know these projects used to be all black, right?"

"No."

"Yes it did, before we were born. It was *mostly* black. When our parents were kids."

"My mom said the same thing," I offered to back Dionna up.

"Just like the projects on Lexington are mostly Puerto

Rican."

"Not all Latinos are Puerto Rican! Dominicans live there too. And Mexicans."

"You ain't gotta OD. Why y'all go crazy if we accidentally confuse y'all? I'm not Puerto Rican, I'm Dominican. Don't call me Puerto Rican." We laughed while Dionna tried out her Spanish accent. She put her hands on her hips and threw her head into a sideways slant. "I'm from the D.R.!"

"You don't want nobody calling you Haitian, or Jamaican do you?"

"I'm not Haitian!" Dionna's eyes grew big and her voice lifted a couple of octaves.

"Puerto Ricans ain't Dominican! They mad loud."

"But y'all all speak Spanish!"

"So!" Ebonee yelled as we stopped in front of Rite Aid.

"Except you!"

They were cutting on each other now. Ebonee smiled a fake, sarcastic smile at Dionna but otherwise, didn't respond to her comment. "We need to get an eyebrow plucker and arch so I can do Jazz's eyebrows. We were *supposed* to do it yesterday!"

"You need to go ahead and buy that relaxer kit and come to my house for a complete makeover."

"She won't even let you get extensions?" Ebonee asked for the ninety-ninth time this year?"

"Let's just get the makeup and go," I said, tired of having the same old conversation with the same old people.

Even your friends think you black and ugly. Soon ain't nobody gonna want to be around YOUR BLACK ASS!

"So, I have a question for y'all," Ebonee began as she fumbled through the eyebrow arches.

"What?"

"I'll be gone until August and I know Shaheem is going to cheat on me."

"Yeah, with one of those Puerto Rican or Dominican girls who think they all that." I couldn't tell if Dionna was joking or not.

"Uh, I am Puerto Rican." Ebonee pushed her hand through her hair and flung it in the air as she announced her ethnicity. "And African American. The best of both worlds."

"See," Dionna said and looked over at me.

"Like you said, there's too many haters in the world. Uh— " Ebonee held up her hand in front of Dionna's face, "—Look in the mirror!"

"Shaheem's gonna cheat on you. And?"

"Should I break up with him now?"

"Do you care if he cheats?"

"Hell yeah!" Ebonee picked up an eyebrow arch. "He said he wants a lap dance for his birthday."

"When is his birthday?"

"In August, when I get back."

"Is he paying you? If he's paying you then give it to him."

"You think I'm a stripper?"

"You might as well be if you give him a lap dance!"

"You stupid."

"I don't do hair for free! So why should you shake your ass for free? What he give you for your birthday?"

"It's hasn't come yet."

"What's he gonna give you?"

"He said he'd give me one for my birthday too."

"Uh huh. You betta make that money! Oh, and I'm telling everybody, my prices are going up since it's summer and I won't get to see everybody every day."

"That's gangsta!"

"No it ain't. Gangsta is giving your stuff away for free!"

"He's my man, Dionna."

"You just said he was a cheater."

"Shut up!"

"I have to go, y'all," Amber said as she sent a text. "My mom's going to get her hair done, and I have to watch my little brother. Jazz, take a picture and text it to me.

"Okay."

Amber left and Dionna and Ebonee went to get some Skittles and iced tea while I waited in line to pay for my makeup and eyebrow arch.

"Did you find out where you'll be working this summer?" Dionna asked as we exited the store and headed home.

"Yeah! At this company that's trying to open a black movie theater."

"Me too! They're on 145th Street, right?"

"Yeah."

"When did you find out?"

"Yesterday!"

"Wait," Ebonee began, "Are they the ones that show movies in the park?"

"Yeah."

"Damn! There be some cute boys out there. One night last summer they had some kids doing poetry, and those boys were fine!"

We cut through the park to get to Mears, and I retraced the steps I'd made every day from kindergarten through fifth grade. As we got closer, I heard some little girls yelling out, 'Hair salon!'

"Whaaaat? No they ain't playing hair salon. I gotta see this," Dionna said as she held us back.

We sat down on the park bench and watched as six little African American and Spanish girls sat against the wall on a 12-inch long slab of concrete that was raised about nine inches from the black rubber safety mat. Other kids were playing on the jungle gym and jetting down the slide while these girls were pretending to do hair.

"Hair salon, hair salon," they each yelled out when all their customers were gone and their make believe chairs were empty. Ebonee, Dionna and I were mesmerized since they looked just like professionals as they pretended to wash each other's hair, gather it up, then style it. One little girl even put on the relaxer, or what would have been relaxer if they hadn't been pretending.

"Hair salon, hair salon."

The best beautician of the bunch, and the one who had the most customers, took one little girl's school uniform sweater, draped it around her chest and made sure it was secure with a quick hand pat before she went to work.

There was absolutely no difference in how these make believe customers sat – heads bent over to one side, necks straining – and the way customers sit when they're getting their hair done for real. The pretend beauticians even sectioned off bits of hair then gathered it together and either put it into a ponytail or braided it, depending on how long it was.

"Look at these little divas," Dionna said. "They starting early."

"Jazz, come on, let's get our hair done."

"I need to get my hair done for real," I said. "I ain't got time for this."

"They're so cute! I'm getting my hair done." Ebonee pulled me up and drug me over to the outdoor salon.

"I'll see y'all later," Dionna said as she got up to leave. Then, just before she left our sight, "Hey, get their names and phone numbers for me!"

"I can do your hair," one girl said the second Ebonee walked over. It was the one who really looked like she could work in any salon in Harlem right now.

"So, what do you have in mind for me," Ebonee asked and flung her long, shiny black hair in the wind.

"Well, let me see," the little girl said. She couldn't have been more than five or six. "Do you like the way you have it now? Cause you can look in the book and see if you want something different."

"That sounds good," Ebonee said and sat in the girl's chair. The five-year-old handed her a make-believe book. Ebonee thumbed her fingers through the air and decided on a style.

All of a sudden, this little Hispanic girl holds up her hands and starts kneading her fingers. "I do massages," she said and smiled at me.

"Ebonee, I'm getting a massage."

"Okay. I'm next."

"I'm Jazz, who are you?"

"Iris. I'm named after my grandmother."

"Nice to meet you, Iris."

"Nice to meet you too," she said and smiled. Her skin was a beautiful beige, her hair was slick, shiny and brown, and the fact that she was missing two front teeth made her even more adorable.

I sat down on the warm rubber mat, and before I could even get comfortable, her little fingers were pressing against my neck. Surprisingly, it felt good! "Do my back, too," I told her since she really seemed to know what she was doing. She worked her way down, and when I felt satisfied, I turned and asked how much.

"One dollar," she said after thinking about it for a second.

Damn! I was just kidding. "Okay," I said and playfully slapped her hand. "One dollar." She smiled again and said thank you. When I got up, about three other girls rushed over to me and starting massaging me again. One little girl even started gently chopping my back like she was a professional. How do they know how to do this, I wondered.

Ebonee was just finishing up. "Do you have a mirror," she asked her stylist. "Yes, that's perfect," she said looking into the invisible mirror her stylist had handed her. "Thank you so much. Can I book an appointment for next month?"

"Yes, if you go up front, the lady up there will do it." These little girls were all up in their make-believe hair salon world. And they were so cute! And having so much fun. Some of them will be doing hair for real by the time they're my age, I predicted.

Ebonee pushed herself up and thanked her stylist.

"Thank you! Bye! I'll see you next month," I yelled as we walked away.

"Okay, see you next month," they yelled back.

"Jasmine!"

I turned around to see Ylenny, Marisol, and Amarylis walking quickly toward us.

"We heard you were looking for us."

I glanced quickly at Ebonee, then back at Ylenny, Marisol at Amarylis.

"I heard you tried to jump Jazz on the train."

"I don't know why you wanna hang out with a liar."

"I don't know why I was hanging out with a racist either, but I was!"

"You supposed to be half Puerto Rican. Why you taking up for her? Lying bitch."

"Who you calling a bitch, bitch! And in case you forgot, I'm Puerto Rican *and* Black, and I can hang out with whoever I want!"

"Ylenny snapped her head in my direction. "Tiara told us you said Latinos were dumb, then you tried to play it off. F___ you bitch, just because you smart. You need to grow some hair. Or get some extensions or something."

"Ahhh shit! Cat fight! Cat fight!" JaVon and Derek had walked up. "

Damn Ebonee, I ain't never seen you fight! Jazz, you just gonna take that!"

"Shut up JaVon!" Ebonee yelled.

"Y'all tripping," Derek said.

"I ain't trying to fight nobody," I said hoping Ylenny would chill.

"Oh you scared now. Yeah! Just like this morning on the train. Now you scared. You weren't scared the other day."

"What y'all fighting about anyway?" JaVon asked. "Wait, somebody was hating on somebody's hair."

"JaVon, shut the f___ up!"

"Wait a minute Ebonee, you know you don't want none of this!" JaVon yelled. Then he broke out in a smile.

"Ain't nobody scared of you," Ebonee said to Ylenny.

"I said her. Hair looking all nappy and crappy!"

"Yup! Yup! Y'all *always* be tripping on each other's hair!"

"Y'all always be tripping on hair!" I screamed.

"Uh oh! Jazz wilding out." JaVon was acting like this was all one big freak show and he was enjoying every minute of it.

"Jazz was right, Ylenny, you do think you all that, you racist bitch."

Ylenny took off her earrings, handed them to Amarylis, and before I knew what was going on, she'd run up to Ebonee and was swinging wildly at her face.

Every part of me froze. Except my stomach which immediately began doing somersaults. Ebonee started swinging back. She hadn't had time to take her earrings off, and one had already landed on the ground. When Ylenny tried to grab Ebonee's hair, Ebonee reached out and grabbed Ylenny's shirt to try to throw her on the ground. She tripped and fell, but Ylenny fell with her. Ebonee rolled on top of Ylenny and started punching her in the face. Derek rushed over to pull Ebonee off while JaVon looked on. But the minute he pulled Ebonee off, Ylenny got up and started swinging. When he let go of Ebonee, Ylenny managed to get a tight grip on Ebonee's hair with both her hands and bring her to the ground.

"Ooooh! I heard something crack," JaVon yelled.

"Stop it! Stop it!"

"You wanna do something," Marisol yelled, daring me to jump in.

"Y'all tripping," Derek said and shook his head.

Ylenny pulled Ebonee's hair as tight as she could, like she was trying to pull it up by the roots. I could see Ebonee wincing, and I felt like I was going to throw up. Ebonee tried to pry Ylenny's hands loose and when she did, Ylenny managed to keep her tight hair grip with one hand, and with her free hand, she started to pummel Ebonee, as fast and as hard as she could on the side of her head.

I ran over and started punching Ylenny in the back of the head, and the next thing I know, I was getting a beat down from Marisol and Amarylis. When it was all over, Derek was holding me around my waist, JaVon had Ylenny in a from-behind bear hug and two men I had never seen before were keeping Marisol and Amarylis from throwing any more punches.

CHAPTER 5

News of the fight had gotten around the school. Even some of the teachers had heard. I didn't know it for sure when I walked into her class, but I suspected Ms. Ervin was one of those teachers.

"Ladies," Ms. Ervin called out to Keyla and Tiana. They didn't stop so she repeated herself using her I-mean-business voice. They got the message. "So, all year I've watched you struggle with each other, especially when it comes to race. I've heard the name calling, you calling each other racist. "

"A lot of kids are," JaVon said.

"A lot of you have no clue what racism is," Ms. Ervin said as she stood up, pulled her chair to the center of the classroom and sat down. "Why do you think I asked those circle questions?"

"So we could stop acting stupid," Sekou said like he thought he was better than everybody else.

"Okay, I get it. Nobody wants to be from Africa. Well, I hate to tell you this— we all come from Africa! African Americans, Dominicans, Haitians, Puerto Ricans."

Raymond's hand shot up. "Ms. Ervin, how you saying that? I'm from D.R."

"She means your ancestors," Sekou answered.

"So, we can deny our ancestry or be ashamed of it, but it's still our ancestry."

"Ms. Ervin you tripping," Raymond said between his

laughter.

Michael raised his hand. "Why do they put African-American on those forms they make us fill out? I don't check that."

"I don't understand." Ms. Ervin looked puzzled.

"I'm not African," Michael answered.

Sekou looked at Michael and shook his head in disbelief. "You're Black, right? Black, African American?" Sekou was trippin' if he thought Michael got what he was trying to say.

"So, Michael, what do you check?" Ms. Ervin asked.

"Other."

"Other?"

"I'm not African!"

Now Ms. Ervin was shaking her head in disbelief. Several hands went up but Ms. Ervin ignored them all.

"I'm not ashamed of my ancestors," Yesenia yelled out.

"So, Yesenia, let me ask you, who are your ancestors?"

"My grandfather who passed, my grandmother and the people who came before them. I don't know who they are, but I'm not ashamed of them."

"And your grandmother is from?"

"Puerto Rico."

"And Puerto Ricans are from?"

"Puerto Rico," we said in unison.

"Puerto Rico and Africa," Tiana said.

"I'm Puerto Rican," Alberto said. "And Ms. Ervin—

"And Spain too," Sekou added.

"—how you gonna say there were slaves in Puerto Rico. We weren't slaves!"

"Okay, okay, Ms. Ervin said and shook her head like she couldn't listen to us anymore. "What I wanna know from all of you is what would happen, if you were to think about and even celebrate the fact that Africans were brilliant and courageous. Not perfect, not without fault, but brilliant and courageous—"

Jocelyn raised her hand to answer, but Ms. Ervin wasn't finished.

"—Instead of thinking of them as these wretched, disgusting people who came from Africa and were enslaved and treated worse than animals get treated?" Ms. Ervin looked as if she were about to cry. I'd never met a teacher who made as many faces or got as excited when they were teaching as Ms. Ervin. After a long silence, she looked over at Jocelyn. "Jocelyn?"

"I think we would be proud of where we came from instead of ashamed."

"But Ms. Ervin, if you live in the hood, it's not like you really want to live there, or be from there," JaVon said and looked around the room. "Who wants to be from a bad neighborhood?"

"The neighborhood is not bad! You're not bad!" Ms. Ervin took a deep breath in and composed herself. "The neighborhood is struggling. Some people in the neighborhood are struggling and some are lost in some respects, but you've got to stop thinking of yourselves as bad, and you've got to understand where all this craziness comes from."

"Then what," Keyla asked.

"Then you stop fighting each other in the streets!"

She had heard. And she was pissed.

"And in school."

"But Ms. Ervin," Keyla protested, "How we supposed to be proud when y'all just say anything to us and treat us any kind of way? You wait, in three days, I'ma curse Ms. Jackson out!"

"Me too," Derek said nodding his head in agreement.

"Always be telling us to get our Black behinds to class. She Black, just like us."

"Okay, we're not going to have that conversation right now. In three days, you'll all be gone—"

"But Ms. Ervin why do some of y'all say stuff like that?"

No he didn't just interrupt her.

"For the same reasons you all say all the crazy things I've been hearing all year. And that's exactly what we're going to discuss today. This madness has been passed down to all of us, however, I'm not going to engage in a discussion about specific teachers or Ms. Jackson." Ms. Ervin glanced quickly at the door. "I grew up, feeling ashamed, just like some of you," she said in a quiet voice.

"Everybody's different, I'm aware of that, but because of all the images we see of Black and Latino people and other people of color, and all the lies written and said about us, it's nearly impossible not to feel shame and to feel like you're not as good as other people. And when you don't feel good about who you are and can't accept who you are—"

Ms. Ervin stopped talking, and she just sat there, staring at us. It's like she wanted to say more, but she either didn't know what to say or she was afraid to say it. Or maybe she was just tired of talking to us. Her diaphragm expanded as she took in a huge gulp of air. It contracted as she exhaled. We sat there watching her, disappointed that she was disappointed in us.

"Jasmine, hand these out please," she said after she'd walked over to her desk and picked up a stack of papers. At the top of the one-page handout were the words: *THE COLOR OF WEALTH* and underneath, the heading: *WHAT IS WEALTH?* "So today we're going to play a game that will help make sense of the handout. Read it over, ask questions as you read, and hopefully, we'll answer them in a few minutes.

WHAT IS WEALTH

In this book, when we use the term "wealth," we mean economic assets. A family's net worth is their assets minus their debts, or what they own minus what they owe. Assets include houses and other real estate, cash, stocks and bonds, pension funds, businesses, and anything else that can be converted into cash, such as cars and works of art.

These are not the only kinds of wealth. Family, social, and community networks, education and skills, public infrastructure and a healthy environment, religion and spirituality: all these not only make us economically more secure, they help us feel well off in ways that money can't buy. But this book focuses on financial wealth, and the story of the government's role in influencing the racial wealth divide.

Our net worth is influenced by the net worth of our parents, grandparents and earlier generations. Most private wealth in the United States was inherited. And even for people who do not inherit money after their parent's death, their family's education and social contacts and financial help from living relatives makes a big difference.

The racial gap has continued to grow (see Figure 1-1). From 1995 to 2001, according to the Federal Reserve Bank, the average family of color saw their net worth fall 17 percent, to $17,100 in just six years while an average white family's net worth grew, 37 percent, to $120,900 in the same period.

The gap in financial assets (cash, stocks, and bonds) is even greater, since most people of color's assets are invested in their home (see Figure 1-2).

Now what? I thought.

"So yesterday I told you that instead of referring to the enslavement of Africans as slavery, it'd be more accurate to call it this massive government work program. So all government programs have names, usually long names that get boiled down into an acronym like Taniff. Taniff, T-A-N-F, stands for Temporary Assistance for Needy Families and TANF is welfare's official name. Welfare used to be a permanent program, but in 1996, our government made it temporary.

"So slavery was meant to be a permanent program, and many people wanted it that way. Others wanted to do away with slavery for differing reasons. We know that it ended, but it was meant to be a permanent way of living in America. So let's use TANF as a model to give slavery a more accurate name. So how would we start it off? Jocelyn?"

"So we should start off by saying permanent assistance?"

"I don't know, let's try it out and see if it works? So, permanent assistance for— for what kind of families?"

"For white families," Sekou said.

"Where these white families needy?"

"They were greedy!"

"JaVon says greedy. Anybody else? Alberto, what do you think?"

"I say for lazy families."

"So, Permanent Assistance for Greedy White Families. Permanent Assistance for Lazy White Families." Ms. Ervin wrote both titles on the white board. "So either PAGWiF or PALWiF." She paused and looked puzzled. "But were all white people lazy back then and were all white people back then greedy? I mean, not all white families enslaved Africans and Jamaicans and, Puerto Ricans and on and on."

Some of us eyed each other with that I-don't-know-what-do-you-think look. Others stared at Ms. Ervin, hoping she'd answer her own question.

"Let's think about that some more in a minute. Right now, let's take a look at the profit that was made from this massive government work program, Permanent Assistance for Greedy White Families or Permanent Assistance for Lazy White Families. When we talk about profit, we're also talking about something called wealth because what this work program did is it made some wealthy for generations to come and it made many, many people poor for generations to come."

"What do you mean, 'for generations'?" Joseph asked.

"Anybody?"

I raised my hand. "It means your grandmother was poor, your mother was poor, now you're poor and it just keeps going."

Ms. Ervin nodded her head. "Sekou?"

"So Ms. Ervin, what you're saying is that we didn't all get the same start."

"Yes."

Xiomara raised her hand. "But all that's changed now, right?"

"Say more, Xiomara."

"I mean, I know it's still people who are mad racist and stuff, but today, you can do anything if you put your mind to it and go to college. 'Cause when my dad came here we were really poor and now he owns his own business."

"Just because your father owns his own business doesn't mean it's not true," JaVon said to Xiomara.

"It just makes me mad when people are always talking about how racist everything is. It's like, Black people say racist things too."

"You can't even talk." Now JaVon was getting heated. "Who stepped in the circle yesterday when she said African Americans are lazy and don't want to work?"

"Not me!"

"Some of the rest of y'all did!"

"Some black people were in there too." Now Jocelyn was throwing in her two cents.

"Yup, some of us stepped in too, JaVon," Brittany said. "I stepped in 'cause I know some people don't do nothing but live off welfare."

"Yup." A few other students agreed and Xiomara nodded her head. Not Sekou. Sekou was pissed. He threw his hands in the air and lashed out at everyone who'd said Black people were lazy.

"Nobody's lazy!"

"I know it's not all black people," Xiomara said. "Just the ones who keep getting welfare and food stamps."

"Like Dominicans don't get food stamps!" JaVon yelled from across the room.

We erupted. Neighborhood street voices belted out. Hands were being waved around in the air. Necks were rolling from side to side. We'd lost all control.

"Shut Up!" Ms. Ervin yelled as she slammed a book so hard onto Jocelyn's desk, it made her jump and almost fall out of her chair. The vibration from the collision between the book and Jocelyn's desktop lingered long afterward, and everybody did just what Ms. Ervin demanded. In a split second, we'd gone from raucous to reverential. All eyes were on Ms. Ervin.

"We are going to have this discussion because a lot of you think you know things you have absolutely no clue about. But we are going to have a discussion, not a brawl, not a smackdown," she yelled. "This is MLK middle school, not Battlefest 2008!"

"Ohhhhhh! Ms. Ervin, whatchu know about Battlefest?"

"Whatchu know about racism and generational wealth!" She looked JaVon dead in the eye. "Not a lot it seems."

"Ooops. She violated you."

"So we're going to learn," Ms. Ervin said, completely ignoring Alberto. Then, she sat down and did her breathing thing where she closed her eyes and took some deep breaths. When she was calm, she opened her eyes and she asked Derek to help her bring the table from the corner of the room.

"We're playing Monopoly?" Alberto asked.

"Sekou, Jasmine, Alberto and Tiana." She motioned for us to sit at the Monopoly game table then handed each of us a baggie filled with play Monopoly money. She also handed each of us the deeds to the properties, all of which already had numerous houses and hotels on them. I even got a *get out of jail free card.*

"Okay now, JaVon, Xiomara and Derek, please, find a seat and join the game." They got up and joined the rest of us.

"So here's what's going down. Sekou, Jasmine, Alberto and Tiana have been playing this game of Monopoly for two hours. JaVon, Xiomara and Derek will now join the game."

"Ms. Ervin," Xiomara began, "there are no more things."

"No more what things?" Ms. Ervin looked at her like she was crazy.

"So I can move. A piece," Xiomara responded as though that should have been obvious.

"No more icons. And?"

Now it was Ms. Ervin's turn. She just stared at Xiomara like she was thinking, '*And? What do you want me to do, I'm not playin'.*

"Find one," someone yelled.

"Use a penny," Jocelyn said.

"Excellent idea," Ms. Ervin said and smiled a fake smile.

"Whaaaat," JaVon said after he had carefully studied the board. "They been playing for two hours, there are no pieces left and they own all the property." He shook his head. "I'm not getting in this game."

"You absolutely are," Ms. Ervin countered. "All of you, find an icon and roll the dice."

"Yeah, son," Sekou said and smiled. "Roll the dice!"

"First give me my money!"

"Yes, how I could forget," Ms. Ervin said and handed JaVon, Xiomara and Derek, fifteen-hundred dollars. "This should help you out.

"Go ahead." JaVon motioned to Xiomara. "Ladies first."

Xiomara rolled the dice and immediately landed on Alberto's property.

"Let's see," Alberto had to check to see how much money he was owed since he already had three hotels and two houses on St. Mark's Place. "Uh, five-hundred dollars," he said and grinned.

"Ms. Ervin, that's not fair. How am I supposed to play if everything is already gone? That's not fair."

"Hold up everybody," Ms. Ervin said and raised her hand in the air. "I have a question for everyone. Xiomara says it's not fair, but every player is playing by the same rules, right?" Why is she yelling, I wondered. "The same Monopoly rules you've always played by. It's true that some people have been playing for two hours and others have just joined the game. But everyone gets a turn, and the rules are the same for everybody playing the game." She looked at Xiomara. "What's your problem?"

Nobody said a word. Xiomara looked like she was about to cry.

"Who's next?" Ms. Ervin asked. "Derek?"

Derek shrugged his shoulders like it was no big deal. "I'll go." He shook the di around in his hand and rolled them onto the board. "Eight. I don't have an icon, so I can't move."

"Oh son, you need an icon, I'll give you an icon." Alberto reached in his pocket and pulled out a torn corner of a Yu-Gi-Oh card.

"Ni— man, get outta here," Derek said and pushed back Alberto's hand. He then reached into his pocket and pulled out a quarter. He counted eight spaces and landed on my property. "How much" he asked.

I'd already figured up what it would cost to land on two of my properties. "Four-hundred fifty dollars," I said and nodded my head. Too bad, I thought, happy I wasn't in his shoes.

"I'm not paying," Derek said and shook his head.

"You been playing for two hours and y'all already own everything, so every time I roll, I'm gonna be owing somebody. Puuhh! I'm not paying." For a minute, nobody said anything.

"Don't worry, son. I can loan you some money. With interest, of course." Alberto grinned just like you do when you know you've done something wrong and gotten away with it. Derek looked like he was contemplating which method he'd use to murder Alberto.

"So Sekou, what was that you said earlier, when we were talking about generational wealth?"

"We didn't all start at the same place."

"So, and I want everyone to think about this, what would happen if this game were to continue— just like it is now, with everybody playing by the same rules, but just like it is now?"

"They'd be my slaves," Alberto said and grinned. "I mean, not like slavery, but basically, yeah, all the money they have, they'd end up giving it to me."

"And me," Sekou added. "And Jasmine and Tiana."

"Um hum, what else?"

No one said anything.

"For JaVon, Xiomara and Derek, where is the safest place to land on this board?" Ms. Ervin asked.

JaVon threw his money on the Monopoly board and grunted. "Jail."

"Really? Jail?" Ms. Ervin asked. JaVon didn't answer.
Ms. Ervin looked at each of us. "So, generational wealth, in this country, is the wealth that slaveholders acquired and passed down to their children who passed it down to their

children. But it wasn't just slaveholders who acquired wealth. Northern bankers became wealthy loaning money to Southern planters. Northern manufacturers took the cotton that was grown in the south and made clothes that they then sold both in the north and the south, and they also became wealthy.

"In fourth grade one day this White kid said, 'Tell your grandfather thanks for this cotton shirt I'm wearing.'"

"What White kid," Keyla asked Derek as if she were going to go jump him.

"When I lived in Brooklyn." Derek tried to play it off like it was no big deal, but I could tell it had been.

"And what did you do?" JaVon asked, demanding to hear that Derek had represented for Black people.

"Okay, he said that," Ms. Ervin said and regained control of the conversation. "But it wasn't just about picking cotton on a plantation in America. Who do you think sailed to Africa and actually traded guns and rum and other cheap products for Africans?" A few of us shrugged our shoulders. "Northern merchants engaged in the slave trade." Ms. Ervin looked around the room. "They became wealthy trading in Africans. Next Tuesday, there's a PBS documentary about one Rhode Island family called *Traces of the Trade,* and I want everyone to watch it."

"What time is it coming on?" I asked.

"Ten o'clock I believe. I'll find out for sure. So, these

traders also built the so called "slave" ships they sailed in, or they had them built, and that opened up a whole new industry. Now if you have all these new workers in the ship building industry, what do you also need?"

No one answered.

"They needed houses to live in, food to eat. So other folk opened up businesses to meet those needs. And again, the bankers loaned them the money to start those businesses. So you have all these people who were profiting and earning money and acquiring assets, some more than others, but all of them were all able to earn a living, while it was illegal for many of your ancestors to earn a living. Those folk were in the game and their children and their children's children were in the game for hundreds of years before ninety-nine percent of the children of those who were enslaved were able to work *and* get paid for the work they did."

"So, what you should've said to that kid is actually, your grandfather owes me and every other African American—" Sekou paused and shrugged his shoulders, "'bout a billion in back pay."

Derek stood up, leaned over and gave Sekou a fist pound.

"Ms. Ervin, what about the slaves— I mean the Africans who got their freedom? And the ones who were already free? Did any of them own businesses or land?" Xiomara asked.

"So, Xiomara, when I talked about the Africans and

Blacks who escaped to Florida, the Maroons—" Ms. Ervin looked around the room to make sure we were still with her. "—Many of them did acquire land and they, oftentimes along with the indigenous who had also run away from the Europeans, founded their own towns. They owned land, had farms, their own communities and eventually some established all-Black towns."

"Seriously?" I asked. I couldn't believe I'd never heard of all-Black towns before. I'd heard of the projects. I'd grown up in the projects where there were mostly Black people, but I never knew Black people used to own so many businesses and that we had our own towns where we were in charge.

"Yes. When Spain still owned Florida, it offered enslaved African men their freedom if they would fight against Great Britain who also wanted to own Florida. And in 1887 Eatonville, Florida became the first incorporated all-Black town in the country."

"Is it still there?" Keyla asked.

"Yup. Eatonville is the oldest all-Black town still in existence. Of one-hundred or so all-Black towns only about twelve are still in existence."

"What happened to the rest?" I asked.

"What happened? So, some towns, like Springfield, Illinois, Rosewood, in Florida – they made a movie about Rosewood many years ago – and Tulsa, Oklahoma, were burned to the ground. Some of the people were murdered in the process, and all of them, obviously, were forced out. But even in cases where there weren't all-Black towns – both during slavery and after it ended – many African Americans had their land taken from them.

"Why?" I asked

"For the same reasons Columbus did what he did," Ms. Ervin answered. "Greed. This notion that I'm entitled to this property, this wealth, and if I want it, I'll take it, by any means necessary. "

"But why would they think they're entitled to it?"

"I don't know," Ms. Ervin said as she shrugged her shoulders. What do you think?" Dionna raised her hand. "Because they thought they were better than Black people."

"Just Black people?" Ms. Ervin asked.

"Indians, too."

"Okay. Who else?" Ms. Ervin looked around the room. room.

"Remember—," she said and threw up her hands "—that whole unit we did on the invasions of Puerto Rico, Cuba and the Dominican Republic? The reasons for the Spanish-American War?"

"Oh yeah," several of us said, all at the same time.

"Everything that happened in Puerto Rico and the Dominican Republican that forced people to leave and come here." Ms. Ervin paused. "This is all related people!"

I shook my head in disgust when I remembered what

we'd learned about why so many Puerto Ricans and
Dominicans started coming here. It was crazy how our
country had gone over there and messed things up for them.
Getting rich while they were suffering.

"Sekou?"

"It's because they thought they were the superior race."

"Or, maybe they just told themselves that to justify their
greed? All the violence?" Ms. Ervin shrugged and looked
around the room. "The wars." She stopped talking and
waited for one of us to challenge what she'd just said.
Nobody did. "So we have these legacies that began with the
formation of our country that say you have one group who
occupies this place in society and all these other groups who
belong somewhere else, and sadly these ideas are still with us
today. But just like it's not true that you're inferior, it's also
not true that White people are superior."

"Pppph!" JaVon slapped at the air. "I don't think that."

"Here in New York City, in the 1800s, Blacks owned
land and had homes where part of Central Park now stands.
You studied this last year, right?"

"No!" Keyla said and looked at Ms. Ervin as if she were
smoking crack or something.

"You didn't learn about Seneca Village?"

"No," we all said as we shook our heads.

"Well, you will," she said as she got up and walked to her
desk.

"No, we won't, not unless you teach us," Keyla said then turned to me and muttered, "You know these White teachers ain't trying to teach us about our history."

"So, we're just now understanding how many people in the south had their land stolen. I believe there are about 107 documented land takings in 13 Southern states." She paused, walked to her desk and flipped through one of her three-ringed binders. "Yes, here it is: *Just in those cases alone – in the south – 406 African American landowners lost more than 24,000 acres of farm and timber land plus 85 smaller properties, including stores and city lots. Today virtually all of this property, valued at tens of millions of dollars, is owned by Whites or by corporations*," she said and closed her binder.

"I want my reparations," Keyla yelled and threw her fist in the air. "Like the old people on 125th be yellin'."

"What's reparations?" Derek asked.

"Reparations refer to money given when someone, or a group usually, has been damaged or hurt. You've heard the saying to make amends?"

"Yes."

"Well giving reparations is when you make amends specifically by paying out money."

"I want my reparations now!" Keyla yelled again.

"Girl, you stupid," Alberto said and shook his head.

"I'm serious!"

"Oh, you claiming slavery now! Now you wanna be from Africa!" JaVon was loud and animated. "You know you woulda been right in the field picking cotton with Derek," he said and burst out laughing. So did everyone else except Ms. Ervin, though she did crack a smile.

The sound of the bell startled me. Ms. Ervin stood and told us not to leave without getting the handouts. "So you have two reading assignments this time, and you've got the whole weekend," she said, "so *do not* come into this class on Monday without having read everything!"

"Tuesday," we all said quickly.

"That's right, you're going to Great Adventure on Monday. Okay. Do not come in this class Tuesday without having read everything! We're going to have a thoughtful, well-informed discussion on Tuesday."

CHAPTER 6

Ms. Jackson was standing at the cafeteria door. She motioned for Ebonee, Dionna, Amber, Keyla and me to stop. "I know what happened yesterday after school. If you even think about starting anything in my lunchroom, every single one of you is going to wish you'd never been born."

As soon as we entered, Keyla mouthed the word "bitch." Then after we were far enough away, "Your parents should have aborted your ass so you'd never been born!"

I looked around for Ylenny and her dogs as we joined the lunch line. Jocelyn and Lenelle were just ahead of us.

"No, we were on food stamps before," Jocelyn said.

"Yeah, a lot of people who get food stamps work," Lenelle added.

"Our parents are the ones working hard over here. And in our family, you're going to college," we heard Jocelyn say. "I mean, we're really not trying to fit the stereotype of Black people."

"Excuse me," Keyla said and threw her voice in Jocelyn's direction. Jocelyn didn't know we were standing behind her. She turned around, and when she saw Keyla, she looked like she'd seen a ghost. "What'd you say?"

"I was talking about how white people have the stereotype that some Black people don't want to go to college—"

"Don't put that on White people! I heard you."

"Trying to lie," I said. I couldn't stand Jocelyn. She was even blacker than me. "Y'all always think you better than everybody else."

"We don't think we're better than you, Jazz."

"Yes you do. You hate us," I said and stared Jocelyn down.

Jocelyn stared back but somehow, her stare was kind. "Jazz, we don't hate you. You hate yourself."

As big as the cafeteria was, Jocelyn's words sucked all the air out of the room and I could no longer breathe. I was like a big round balloon one minute, then, as if someone had stuck a pin in me, flat and lifeless the next.

"Ladies, is there a problem?" Ms. Jackson had snuck up behind us. "I said, is there a problem?"

"No," Keyla said in as nasty a voice as she could conjure up.

A slow silent tear began making its way down the side of my face, and I turned and walked just as slowly out of the cafeteria. There's no way that bitch was going to send me running twice in one week.

"Don't listen to her," Ebonee said as she walked up from behind and put her arms around me. "Bitch!"

We walked to the stairwell leading up to the first floor and sat down on the steps.

"Jazz, forget her. She don't know you."

The stairwell door opened.

"What's wrong now?" It was Ms. Ervin. "Ebonee, what happened?"

"Jocelyn and her stupid ass."

"Jasmine—"

I leapt up before Ms. Ervin could summon me to her room. Ebonee ran after me. She grabbed my armed just as I reached for the cafeteria door.

"Jazz forget Jocelyn! She's not worth it."

"Okay! I can wait until school is out," I yelled as I wrenched my arm away from her.

"You're not fighting Jocelyn!" Ebonee was yelling now.

"I know I'm not! We are."

"I'm not getting into another fight."

"Why not?"

"Because I don't have beef with Jocelyn. We need to stop fighting each other anyway, like Ms. Ervin said."

"Ms. Ervin don't know what we go through."

"Well, if you wanna start something go ahead. Just make sure you can finish it."

"You don't know either!"

"Know what?"

"What I go through!"

"What are you talking about?"

"Forget it," I said and walked away.

"Jazz!"

I ignored Ebonee and kept walking.

During the last two periods of class, I alternated between trying to sleep and writing in my journal.

> *You tell me to be proud*
> *You're beautiful some say*
> *Then why do all the boys*
> *Look the other way*
> *I wish my hair were long*
> *And straight and soft and good*
> *My mom doesn't understand,*
> *But I really wish she would*
> *I know that I'm not ugly*
> *But I'm not*

I couldn't finish the sentence. In one instant, my skinny little one-hundred pound self felt like it weighed three-hundred pounds. I didn't have enough energy to hold my head up. I would've fallen asleep if my phone hadn't vibrated. It was Ebonee telling me to come to her rehearsal after school. The eighth-graders in the drama club had written a musical about our school, and Ebonee was singing a song she'd composed. Since we were going to Great Adventure on Monday, today would be their next to last rehearsal. I still couldn't believe she turned down a chance to go to LaGuardia.

I put my head back down on the desk and closed my eyes. I saw me and Ebonee when we were ten. We were both in our pajamas. I was spending the weekend at her house because my parents were out of town at a funeral. We got to stay up late and watch scary movies, but before we watched movies, Ebonee and her five-year-old sister, Roneisha, put on a talent show. They were both singing into a hair brush pretending they were Destiny's Child, Minus One. Roneisha kept saying, "no, not Destiny's Child, Destiny's Child Minus One because there's only two of us."

Even though I loved spending the night at Ebonee's, being her best friend was like having a crush on somebody who didn't even know you existed. You felt happy and depressed at the same time. Kids were so evil to me and so nice to her, even though they knew we were best friends. I'll never forget in third grade the time Shayna invited everyone to her birthday party except me. When Ebonee found out, she told her mom she wasn't going, and she and I had our own house party. We took pictures and took them to school to show Shayna how much fun we had at our own party!

I peeked out at the clock. Fifteen more long minutes. I wondered what we were having for dinner. I wondered what it would be like living in an all-black town. Maybe back then it was mad cool, but I couldn't imagine how it would be any fun now. Maybe if we were all one color.

I closed my eyes and saw me and Ebonee in her apartment last night. We were both fixing our faces. Her head was throbbing and she had tears in her eyes as she stared at herself in the mirror. Ylenny hadn't left any physical bruises, but when you get punched like that and when your hair is almost ripped out of your scalp, your confidence is bruised. And even though Ebonee got some punches in, I could tell she felt ashamed getting beat on the head like that.

I saw Derek holding me and asking me if I was okay. That was weird since I'd never heard of a guy trying to break up a fight between two girls before. I saw the group of boys who walked by me on the way home from school last month. 'Damn, she black as my hoodie,' one said as they approached. Why could boys be black and it didn't matter? Why did we have to look a certain way? And the ones who did date dark-skinned girls didn't want anybody to know.

I raised my head and began writing again. *Everything is falling apart. Why doesn't she have my back? Why don't boys like me?* I stopped writing with my right hand and began writing with my left hand like I'd done for the homework Ms. Ervin gave us. *Because they don't know you. They don't even see you. They don't know you're there.* I transferred the pen back to my right hand. *When are they gonna start seeing me?* Then back to my left. *When you want them to. When you stop being ashamed of you.* My phone vibrated again.

"R u coming?"

I continued to write. *Things would have been so much easier if I'd come out like Dalani. Maybe you should go to LaGuardia. It's not like things are gonna get any better. You're crazy not to go. The best performing arts high school in the world! You need to have more confidence in yourself.*

I left school and went straight home. We didn't have dance class on Fridays, and I wouldn't have felt like going anyway. I was exhausted and needed to go to bed. My mom wasn't having it. The minute I walked into the kitchen, she confronted me. Ms. Ervin had called her and told her everything. She told her about the fight last night and that something had happened with Jocelyn today. She said we were gonna talk. Now!

Okay," I said. *Good!* And before she could start, I asked her if my father married her because she was light-skinned.

"What?" My mom looked at me with a stare so menacing I should have grabbed my cell phone, ran into my room and dialed 911. She was starting to burn a hole through me, but by now, I didn't care. I told her everything about how kids used to tease me because I was dark-skinned. About being knocked down by Gavin. She said she thought they were teasing me because I was smart.

"That's what I told you," I said. Then, I told her about the prom and about hating the fifth grade because I got teased so much.

"Are you angry with me because you father is dark-skinned?" At first, I didn't answer her. I just stared at my lap.

"No. But when I grow up, I wanna marry somebody Spanish or White so my kids' hair won't be kinky like mine."

She rested her forehead in her hand and propped her elbow on the table. Her chest began to heave, and I could feel the vibration in the table. She took short, shallow breaths and sounded just like a dog panting. I slumped down in the chair and tried to tune her out. After a long minute, she got up and blew her nose.

"I don't know where you're getting all this self-hatred from all of a sudden, but you need to stop looking at all your friends and all these girls on TV. So these little ignorant children teased you in the fifth grade. I bet some of them teasing you were just as dark as you are. Weren't they?"

Stop yelling, I wanted to say. "No. I mean, sometimes. Some of them were."

"We got enough people out here trying to make life miserable for people. I'm not going to have you growing up hating anybody because they're light-skinned or dark-skinned or whatever skinned!" My mom stopped just long enough to take a deep breath in and start up again. "Ms. Ervin told me about this fight you were in – you and Ebonee. And now you wanna fight another girl?"

What? How she know that?

"I'm calling your grandmother. You're going down to South Carolina as soon as school is out. You need to get away from all this stupidity. And you not fighting anybody. You hear me?"

It was my time to wear the menacing stare. *I can't believe this shit! You think I'm a hater when I just told you it was all those other kids hatin' on me? Send me down early. I haven't seen my grandmother in three years. I bet she won't think I'm a hater!*

We both waited out the silence. Finally, I nodded yes. She went back to cooking dinner, and I walked out, went to my room and slammed the door. Five seconds later, she was opening my door with one hand and holding a large spoon in her other hand.

"Since you wanna slam the door, you can go vacuum the living room."

"I'ma do it tomorrow."

"You're gonna do it right now! And while you're vacuuming, you can calm yourself and act like you got some sense."

I got up, retrieved the vacuum cleaner out of the closet and immediately began plotting my revenge. I turned over the phrases in my head as I maneuvered the vacuum cleaner under the table and around the couch. *I want it to rhyme. I want everybody to read it and hold their breath for a second while they cover their mouths with their hands.*

I didn't stop vacuuming until my mom said it was time to eat. I knew she'd give me something else to do if I finished sooner. We usually cleaned the house on Saturday, and I wasn't about to spend a Friday night mopping and cleaning up the bathroom.

While we ate, my mom told me we had to reschedule the sleepover with Aunt Angie. She said Aunt Angie had to fill in for someone at a seminar during the day and she'd be too tired to be much fun tomorrow night. She said we'd do it when I came back from South Carolina. I didn't even care about the sleepover anymore — now that I knew my own mother was against me. And I'm sure Aunt Angie would side with her. But how could they understand, I thought. They're both light-skinned!

After we ate, I washed the dishes and put them away. Once I heard my mom close her bedroom door, I locked myself in my room and logged on to AIM. I entered my username, *kisskiss94@hotmail.com,* then my password. I hit the connect button and began typing.

> *Get on a boat and go back to Haiti.*
> *We got enough cockroaches in New York City!*
> *Don't need to name names, you know who you are*
> *Ugly as sin and blacker than tar*

Not more than thirty seconds after I'd pressed send, my phone rang.

"Why are you doing this?"

Before I could respond, the words "Name names since y'all both black and ugly!" popped up in the chat line. S*exyhot318* had posted it.

"See. This whole thing is getting out of hand."

I sat there, stunned, staring at the computer as tears made railroad tracks down the sides of my face. I hung up on Ebonee, pushed my chair back and threw myself onto my bed. I smothered myself in my pillow and tried to forget about everything that had happened today, yesterday and all this week.

I needed to go away in my head to someplace different.

Someplace I'd never been before. Ebonee called right back as I lay there trying to escape. A few seconds later, my phone beeped letting me know I had a text message. I took off my shoes, and with all my clothes on, got into bed, pulled the covers over my head and went to sleep.

The next morning, I read Ebonee's text. She told me it was okay I didn't come to rehearsal, but I had to come to a party for her cousins on Saturday night. She'd been excited about them coming all week. They were her first cousins on her real father's side and she'd never met them before. "I've had enough of Puerto Ricans for one week," I muttered out loud, "so no, I don't want to go your party!" I texted her back and reminded her that I had a sleepover at Aunt Angie's, even though it had been cancelled. She texted me back wanting to know if I wanted to go with them to the Puerto Rican Day parade. This would be Ebonee's first time going and her cousin's too. I definitely wasn't going to any parade.

I spent the rest of the weekend sleeping, watching TV, and staying away from my mother. When I didn't hear from Ebonee again, I figured she was having too much fun to be bothered with me. On Sunday night, I took a look at the handouts Ms. Ervin had given us. What? Nineteen pages? I know she doesn't expect us to read all of this, not with four days left in school.

As soon as I began reading the first handout, I wondered

if anyone else had read it and what they were thinking. Onesimus was a slave and a medical pioneer, it said. He developed a vaccine for smallpox back in the 1700s. There was another handout about Sampson, another enslaved African in South Carolina who made a cure for snake bites. His cure was so successful that the governor of South Carolina gave him one-hundred dollars a year for the rest of his life and granted him his freedom.

Damn, I thought. They never talk about these people when they teach us about slavery. All we hear about is Frederick Douglass and Harriet Tubman and all the people who got beaten and hanged. She'd given us two stories written by former slaves. They were interviewed when they were in their '60s and '80s (one woman was one-hundred) and they talked about their lives when they were enslaved.

One man, Gus Smith, even talked about his grandfather being an old fashioned herb doctor. A doctor really since his cures worked better than the White doctor's whose cures didn't work. He had even saved Gus's life when he had typhoid fever and pneumonia when he was nineteen. But that's the good part. The rest of what they wrote— all I could do was shake my head. One slave master was so mean, he killed his own son because he stayed out late one night. He beat him to death, just like he'd beat the Africans who worked for him every morning. Gus said that that was their breakfast – a beating. Before that, though, he'd killed a seventy-year-old woman. He wouldn't give her any food because he was just stingy with his food, and she was so hungry that she stole a chicken and started cooking it in her cabin. When he found out, he made her eat the whole thing, boiling hot, right out of the pot and she died on the spot.

I didn't really want to read anymore, but I couldn't stop. Gus Smith said that 'in the time of slavery, people were sold like cattle or hogs.' Those words kept going around and around in my head, like a stupid song that you know is stupid but you can't stop singing. 'People were sold like cattle or hogs, cattle or hogs, cattle or hogs.' And Ms. Ervin was right. We didn't start off in the same place. When the people got their freedom, over and over again they talked about not even having any underwear. They just left the plantation with barely any clothes, no shoes, and then they had to try to find work and a place to live.

One man, I think it was Gus, got lucky since his owner gave Gus's father part of his land to farm for five years. After five years, he said that whatever he cleared, he could then take half for himself. They ended up with fifty acres and they basically had a farm where their family raised their own sheep and grew cotton, and he said his mother made their clothes from the cotton they grew. But then there were the stories of the people who got their freedom and their owners said they could stay on and work but they weren't going to pay them if they did. I opened up my journal and wrote *sold like cattle or hogs.*

I looked up the dictionary definition of slavery online. Every definition began with the words, drudgery and toil. The second definition said, *submission to a dominating influence*, and the third one said, *the state of a person who is chattel of another.* Ms. Ervin had said that chattel meant property. There was an example that used the word in a sentence: *a child born into slavery was considered simply another addition to the master's wealth and property.* That's what Gus was saying. And that's what Ms. Ervin was trying to get us to understand. I opened up a blank document and typed my own definiton.

Slavery (noun)

A period in America before the Civil war where Black people could be sold like cattle or hogs, where six-year-old children could be ripped from their mothers arms and as many as twelve children could be sold away from their mother in one day, *if it was profitable*, and where a woman could be sold six times or beaten until her blood-soaked shirt stuck to her back after her master had someone else pour salt on her open wounds, and where the people were fed their food in a trough, next to the hogs, but where some received what they said was good care *since "they were as particular with the slaves as with the stock—that was their money, you know."*

I'd had enough of slavery for one night. Just even looking at the pictures. Their hair was either nappy and all over the place, or they had a rag tied around it. And they looked so tired. Nobody was smiling. Some of their faces were dusty and others were shiny for some reason. And they were all so black!

You so black! No wonder boys don't see you. Especially at night!

CHAPTER 7

I woke up on Monday contemplating whether I should even go to Great Adventure. I didn't know if I wanted to be around Ebonee, or Dionna and Amber either for that matter. I'd gone to Great Adventure when we were little, but I didn't remember much about the trip. After lying in the bed for what seemed like a long time, I got up, got dressed and headed out the door. My mom called me back to make sure I had enough money. She probably feels guilty, I thought, for calling me a hater.

Great Adventure turned out to be too much fun! Ebonee, Dionna, Amber and I tried our hardest to ride every ride— twice! That morning, when I saw Ebonee, we hugged and she asked me if I was still mad.

"Mad at you?"

"Mad at whatever you were mad at. Jocelyn, me, whatever."

At first, I didn't answer her. I didn't want to talk about it with her because I didn't think she understood. "I get it," I said finally. "You just wanna do you."

She shook her head and said we needed to forget about it and just have fun at Great Adventure. She said we'd talk before she left town.

* * *

Tuesday was uneventful except for our discussion of the readings Ms. Ervin had given us. She said they were wrongly called slave narratives. She said she hoped that by reading them we could really see that the people who wrote them were real people with families and thoughts and ideas about their lives and their situation. In one narrative, a slave master fell and broke his hip. He knew he was going to die so he told the people who were working for him where he'd hidden all his money. He felt guilty about enslaving them and he wanted to try to pay them back. But they told the overseer and, of course, he went and found the money but told them he hadn't.

"But why did they tell the overseer?" Derek couldn't believe it.

"Anybody?" Ms. Ervin wanted us to talk to each other.

"They were afraid," Jocelyn said.

"But he was dead!" Derek still couldn't understand why they'd tell him when they knew he would keep the money for himself.

"So, the overseer's job was what? To keep the workers in a constant state of fear so they wouldn't rise up and take their freedom. So they'd continue to do as they were told. Right?"

"Yeah," Xiomara began, "I read where the master whipped one woman or man, I can't remember, and he made the other slaves, I mean their family members, pour salt on their wounds."

"So class, slavery was a business enterprise and in order to keep Africans and Blacks enslaved, their masters beat them, they threatened them, they made examples of them."

"How?"

"They cut off the hands and feet of those who tried to escape to show others what would happen if they tried the same thing. They filled them with so much fear that they were able to force them into doing things they didn't want to do and keep them working. And just because their master died or even when slavery ended, that fear doesn't automatically disappear."

I looked around to see several students eyeing each other and shaking their heads. Last year when we talked about slavery, a lot of people kept saying how they wouldn't have been slaves 'cause they would have killed the slave masters and run away. But when you read how it really was... Alberto was so stupid, he didn't even realize the slave narratives were real. I needed for us to change the subject.

"So, what's everyone doing over the summer?" I wanted to raise my hand and ask. I couldn't wait to get out of New York and go see my grandmother.

We had just ten minutes left in the period when Sekou opened his big mouth. "Didn't light-skinned people get treated better during slavery?"

"So, let's go back to the readings," Ms. Ervin said. "There are thousands of narratives written by people who were enslaved. Some wrote entire books. And we don't find anywhere in their narratives, or in any other writings, that light-skinned people, in the United States, were routinely treated better during slavery.

"And as much as we like to joke about who worked in the big house and who worked in the field, no matter how light or dark you were, if you were working inside, you were on call twenty-four seven. So, if your master's child woke up at three in the morning, sick with a fever, you woke up at three in the morning.

"Now it is true that the master's children, born of rape, were often light-skinned and sometimes they received special treatment like being granted their freedom when they turned eighteen or twenty-one."

"That's messed up," Keyla said and shook her head.

"So, during slavery you did have enslaved Africans and Blacks and free Africans and Blacks, and many of the free lighter-skinned people didn't want to be associated with their darker skinned brothers and sisters who were enslaved because they were trying to have a better life. When slavery was over, and all Blacks were free, Whites did treat lighter skinned Blacks differently. There were even Black people light enough to be taken for White, and many lived their lives as White people, long after slavery ended."

Keyla raised her hand. "Light-skinned people are still

treated better a lot of times."

"No we're not!"

No Brittany ain't trying to get an attitude. Acting like she don't know it's true.

"Yeah, y'all are!"

"Unfortunately—," Ms. Ervin said and held up her hand like she was a school crossing guard, "—that legacy is still with us."

Yesenia raised her hand. "Even in Puerto Rican families, my parents and even my grandparents didn't want my mom to marry a dark-skinned man."

"Mejorar la raza," Xiomara said.

"What?" Keyla asked.

"It means you have to better the race," she said and paused. "By marrying someone lighter."

"That's OD," Joseph said and shook his head. Other kids shook their heads too, but didn't say anything.

"But y'all already light," JaVon said.

Tiara raised her hand. "My mom said when she was growing up – my mom is really light – she said my titi used to be so mean to her and she never understood why. But now she says it's because my titi was jealous 'cause my mom is the lightest of all the kids, and everybody else is more like Brittany's color 'cause Puerto Ricans can be from the same family and be all different colors. But my mom said she didn't even realize why my titi was so mean."

"You see what I mean when I say we keep passing this

stuff down?" Ms. Ervin's question silenced us all. I was starting to feel sick. I felt even worse when she told us that during slavery, White people looked at dark skin like it was something evil, and they referred to our hair as wool. She said that because of this, we started to find ways to straighten our kinky hair— during slavery! Or wear wigs to hide it. Or cut it so short the kinks became invisible. She also said Black people used to pinch their noses.

Then she read from a newspaper article titled "White is Beautiful" where a Black teacher in Brooklyn wrote that Black people seemed to despise themselves and anything that looked like them. He also said that when he showed some Black girls a Black doll, they started screaming and scampering. The article was written in *Frederick Douglass' Paper.* In 1853!"

The room was silent. Like we were taking a test. Nobody said a word.

"Do you think in 1853, folk in Africa were over there dissin' each other's hair?" Ms. Ervin paused. I could feel my heart beating. "Oooh girl, you betta do something 'bout that wool!" A few kids laughed, but nothing she was saying was funny. "Or cutting it off because they thought it looked bad? Do you think your ancestors spent time hating on each other's dark skin?"

Some kids whispered their no. Others shook their heads no. I didn't speak or nod because, just like last week in the cafeteria, I could no longer breathe. I felt like everyone was staring at me like I'd done something wrong, and they were waiting for me to confess. I became as still as a corpse as I tried to will myself invisible. I wanted to vanish into the air like in a Sci-Fi movie when you needed to escape the evil that was chasing you – quickly catching up to you – so it could kill you dead.

I heard Ms. Ervin announce that she'd invited our parents to class Thursday for an end-of-unit ceremony. She wanted us to bring pictures of our parents, grandparents, foster parents, whoever was important to us, to the ceremony. I begged God to just make the bell ring.

* * *

On Wednesday, I slept through English, and in Science, all we did was help Ms. Ringwuld clean up and put away the equipment for the summer. In Algebra, we had a sub, and as usual, everybody went crazy. One group of kids actually had a dance party. Constance started doing the stripper dance, and Anthony got up and started bumping butts with her. Other kids joined in and soon, half the class was bouncing and clapping and bumping butts. Of course, the sub came over and shut it down. I folded my arms across my desk, buried my head and tried to tune out everybody. It was impossible to tune out Malcolm, Derek and Vincent since they were standing up right next to my desk.

"At least people in Brooklyn, they rob for good stuff like the Chinese Take Out Man. Niggas in the Bronx, they steal your shoes," Vincent said and shook his head.

"Nah son, my cousin lives in Brooklyn, and Brooklyn niggas be carrying machetes and chopping off hands and feet and shit. It's like every time they leave, they leave with some type of body part." Malcolm lived in the Bronx but he used his father's address so he could go to school in Harlem. He'd been left back a couple of times and was fifteen in the eighth grade. I wish he'd stayed in the Bronx.

"Nah son, the Bronx is worse," Derek said convinced he was right. "You always get jumped in the Bronx. And robbed."

"That's the problem mynigga." Malcolm lowered his voice and moved in closer to Vincent and Derek. "Who in they right mind goes to the store to buy an iPhone 3G nowadays? Who does that? You just go up on Grand Concourse, and you walk up to a nigga and start talking. Then— BOOM!" Malcolm threw a knock-out punch in the air. "You should know if some nigga comes up and starts a conversation, something's up."

I shook my head and counted the minutes before it was time for Ms. Ervin's class. When the bell rang, I bolted for the door and headed straight to Social Studies. As soon as we sat down, Ms. Ervin showed us a series of film clips. When the fifth period bell rang and it was time for lunch, nobody wanted to leave. Everybody wanted to see the whole thing again. We were still talking about it when Ebonee walked up.

"You didn't say you were having a party today."

"You should've seen it," I said and tried to imitate one of the dance moves I'd just seen. Then I remembered I was still mad at Ebonee. She said we'd talk before she left town. Part of me wanted to talk, but the other part dreaded talking to her the same way you dread taking a test you know you're not prepared for. I was afraid. Afraid of what she might say. Of what I might say.

"They danced just like we do," Sekou said still hyped.

"Who?" Ebonee asked.

"Ms. Ervin showed us this film about the slaves— Africans who were enslaved—" Sekou caught himself, "—and how they sang work songs to get through the day. But also how Africans from a long time ago danced. Just like we do, son!"

"And in slavery, they be doing the hambone," Keyla said as she began slapping her thigh and acting crazy.

"Yeah," Tiana said, "after they outlawed the drum."

"That ain't no hambone, that's some hippopotamus thigh bone shit."

"Nigga you wish you could get some of these hippopotamus thighs."

I never understood why Keyla didn't get upset when JaVon joked about how big she was.

"Word, dog, they had songs where they told you what dance steps to do, too." I'd never seen Derek this animated. "Just like the Cupid Shuffle."

"What about those little kids in Africa, doing the same shit we do over here. Mynigga, that shit was ti-ight!"

"And what about the Walkaround? That shit was just like Battlefest!"

"I know right," Dionna said.

"That Elegba dance, damn, they looked just like Beyonce," Sekou said.

"No they didn't," Keyla said and looked at Sekou like he was crazy.

"They danced like Beyonce!"

"Yeah, son, 'cause they didn't look nothing like Beyonce," JaVon said.

"Why y'all so hyped about redbone girls anyway?" Keyla asked.

Yeah, why are you? I wanted to stab JaVon. I wanted to stab Anthony. I wanted to stab all the boys who thought they couldn't see me. Because I wasn't light-skinned like the Spanish girls. Or caramel like Ebonee.

"The women, danced like Beyonce—," Tiana began,

"I like all women!" JaVon answered.

"Yeah right," Keyla said and shot JaVon the evil eye.

"—but when the men were doing the, how do you say it, Ele—?"

"Ay-leg-buh."

"—Elegba dance, they looked just like my sister's step team in high school. It was the same moves."

"What high school has a step team?" Jocelyn wanted to know.

"It's a private school. Middle Passage."

"Naw seriously, I don't discriminate, redbone, hambone, hippopotamus bone, it's all the same to me."

"Dead ass, you got one more time to say that shit!"

"And what?" JaVon was taking this way too far. I could see Keyla getting upset.

"And I'ma beat your Black ass all over this lunchroom." Our table got quiet.

"Chill. I was just joking."

"Ah hah, and you need to quit," Dionna said. "You always take it too far."

"So that's all y'all did was watch a film?" Ebonee asked.

"Yeah, so we could see our ancestors weren't just slaves," I answered. "Enslaved."

"What about what she asked us to think about?" Jocelyn asked.

"And that Primus lady—" Keyla got up and tried, but didn't even come close to dancing like the woman in the video. "—She was no joke!"

Jocelyn repeated her question. "What about what Ms. Ervin asked us to think about?"

"Think about what?" Sekou asked.

"About comparing our music today with the music back then."

"Nah, nah," JaVon began. "They were talking about having sex, too. You remember last marking period when she told us about that nigga, Jelly Roll Morton, so don't even try that."

"That's not what she said."

"What she say then?"

"She said, yeah there were songs about sex, but they weren't saying stuff like, 'Can I suck it, can I eff it' and stupid stuff like they show on TV."

"Yeah!" Keyla yelled.

"They weren't calling women bitches. They were trying to get through slavery—"

"I'm talking about after slavery when—"

"—Yeah!" Tiana interrupted. "Remember she played that song, *Ne Le Pege A La Negra*, about the slave— the man who told his master to stop beating his woman."

"Compare that with *Ask Them Hoes!*" Jocelyn shrugged her shoulders and held up her hands as if to say, how does that make any sense?

"That's right!" Keyla yelled again. "Because they were making them have sex just to get more slaves." Jocelyn gave Keyla the evil eye. Keyla gave it right back to her. I wished she would've slapped her. "You know what I mean," she said. "So they could have children who were slaves. Uhhhh!" Keyla slapped herself hard on the thigh. "HE MADE THEM HAVE SEX SO HE COULD HAVE MORE PEOPLE—" She stopped and gave Jocelyn gave her best *"you satisfied!"* face. "—working for him for free without getting paid a damn thing, and they didn't have no rights, and they treated them like animals even though they weren't. THEY WERE HUMAN BEINGS!"

"Go Keyla, go Keyla!" Everybody began clapping and bouncing from side to side. Like we were at a party. "Go Keyla, go Keyla." Keyla waved her arms in the air and bounced her head up and down as she sucked up all the applause. Then she came back to earth.

"I'ma be honest with y'all though, that one song got to me."

"What song?" Tiana asked.

"The one about the auction block."

"Yeah! Me too."

"It was just something about it. Like you felt something when they were singing."

"What you feel? You felt like you was a slave?" JaVon was being stupid again.

"No, dumbass. Like what they said, no mo' a that shit! And ohhhh, the one thing—"

"Stop!"

"—We did wrong!"

"Stop!"

"Was stayed in the wilderness way to long!"

"Your ass is in the wilderness now."

"And ohhhh—"

"Mynigga, dead ass, you cannot sing!"

"—The one thing that we did right! Was the day we began to fight!" Keyla stopped singing *No More Auction Block For Me* and ended her performance with a call to action. "Let's go demand our rights! We want our reparations."

"Yeah, you go outside yelling that. You'll get your reparations all right. The cops be done locked your ass up so fast, you won't even have time to call home. We'll be running after you in the police car yelling, Keyla, Keyla, we'll bail you out."

"No, it'll be like in that movie when they took one sister away, Dionna will be yelling, 'Write! Write!'"

"Y'all are some ignorant niggas," Ebonee said in between her laughter.

"Yeah, you'll be locked up just like Derek was last summer," JaVon said.

"You were locked up?" I asked him.

"Yup."

"For real?"

"Yup."

"Why?"

"Walking down the street," he said and shrugged his shoulders.

"You know how they just come up and frisk you for no reason, thinking you got drugs," JaVon said.

"You had drugs on you?"

Derek just looked at me and shook his head.

"You know Derek don't do drugs! His dad won't let him," JaVon said and laughed.

"Then why'd they lock you up?"

"Nah, they started searching me and I went off. Then they handcuffed me and put me in the car." Again, Derek shrugged his shoulders like it had been no big deal.

"Are you serious?" Tiana asked.

"Were you scared?" I asked.

"Nah! I was mad crazy." Derek lowered his voice and we watched as his whole body morphed into someone who didn't want to remember something he could never forget.

"You know that kid who got shot last year?"

"Sean Bell?" I asked.

"Nah, in White Plains—"

"Sean Bell was two years ago," JaVon said.

"Sean Bell, the one the cops shot at his bachelor party?" Keyla asked.

"After he left the party. They shot him fifty times."

"I remember that! He was getting married the next day. And didn't they already have kids?"

"Yeah. Not Sean Bell, another one."

"—Rayshaun Carmichael," Derek said. "He was my cousin, but he was like a brother to me." Derek paused, averted his eyes for several seconds, then looked up at me.

"That messed me up."

"You never said he was your cousin."

"I know." Again, he looked away – this time, shaking his head at the pointlessness of it all.

"He got shot over break, right?"

"Yeah."

"Is that what made your personality change?" Ebonee asked.

"What?" Derek looked puzzled.

"You hardly talk anymore."

Derek shrugged his shoulders and stared at the floor. Now I was shaking my head. "I mean, you weren't scared?"

"When they first came up on me, I was scared. But when they put their hands on me, I started wilding out. I was cursing and screaming for them to get the f___ away from me."

"Derek, you could've gotten killed."

"I wasn't even thinking about that. All I was thinking about was Rayshaun and how I wished I had a gun so I could shoot them the way they shot him. Murderers."

"Son, that's OD" Sekou said and shook his head. "I probably would've done the same thing."

"Son, you're an honor student," JaVon said. "You know we can't have you going to jail."

"Oh, it's gonna happen," Derek said. "He's going get locked
up for something somewhere down the line, whether he did it or not."

"They already frisked me a few months ago. Me and my cousin."

"I know. They come up on you and start patting you down like you a criminal. How can they do that?" JaVon asked. "Just 'cause we hanging out on the corner? They don't even ask no more they just come up and start patting you down. We raise our arms in the air and turn around before they even get to us."

"And they be dumb tight when you ain't got no drugs."

"Yup."

"Mynigga, get used to it. You're in Harlem, son," Derek said. "Get used to it!"

Why should he have to get used to it, I asked but kept the question to myself. I remembered this article about a college student from Harvard who got locked up. He was going to law school and he already had like, two degrees from Columbia and NYU, and they still locked him up. He had just gotten back from India, and when he told his lawyer, she thought he was crazy. She was like, Harvard? You just got back from India? Okay, we'll get you some help.

Like he was delusional! Only he wasn't delusional. He was Black, though. He only got off when the prosecutor said he knew him because he was in his class the year before, AT HARVARD! If they lock up somebody who went to Harvard for just walking down the street, they'll lock up anybody.

"You know they have a quota," Jocelyn said. "They have to do so many during their shift or else. My uncle is a cop, and he said he hates it, but they make them do it! They're supposed to make up charges to get their numbers up."

"So how is that any different from slavery when the overlookers—"

"Overlookers?" JaVon asked.

"—Or drivers or whatever Ms. Ervin said."

"You mean the overseers."

"She said the overseers were White but sometimes they made one slave— one African keep the other Africans in check. The overlookers."

"Yeah! Or when they made one pour salt on someone else's back?" Tiana yelled.

"We not talking about no slavery right now," JaVon said as he swatted violently at the air. "We're trying to remember the positive aspects of our ancestors' lives." He sat up straight and puffed out his chest.

"Who you supposed to be?" For the thousandth time this year, Keyla and JaVon were about to start cutting on each other. All eyes were on him waiting to see what he'd come back with.

"Do you ever think you might not make it?"

Everybody froze. Sekou's question had snuck up from behind like a gangsta on the street intent on taking us out.

Now all eyes were on him. "It's like, we always getting shot by the cops or somebody from our neighborhood."

"Mynigga, ain't nobody getting shot!"

"Yeah, but do you think about it?"

Before JaVon could answer, the bell propelled us out of our seats and on to sixth period. "What about those little kids?" Anthony yelled, competing with about one-hundred-and-fifty MLK seventh and eighth-graders making their boisterous exit out of the lunch room. "Dog, that shit was tight!"

Sekou pushed back his chair and hoisted his backpack into place. JaVon stood up with him, reached his arm around Sekou then planted his hand on Sekou's shoulder. "Son, don't worry. I got ya back."

I wish Ebonee would put her arms around me and tell me she had my back. I wish it were tomorrow. Two more periods today, then seven tomorrow. After that, no more middle school. Ever.

CHAPTER 8

I walked into Ms. Ervin's room for the very last time, and it looked as if I'd stepped inside a rainbow. Purple and white and yellow and green and red chiffon cloth hung from the ceiling. The desks and chairs were pushed to the perimeter of the room leaving a large open space in the middle. A red carpet stretched from one end of the classroom to the other. Purple and white chiffon cloth hung over the small book case placed against the back wall. Three white candles, a sea of purple and white sapphire gem stones and a bouquet of peace lilies sat on top of the bookcase that had been turned into an altar.

"Ms. Ervin, we gonna pray for somebody today?" Sierra asked as soon as she spotted the altar. "I thought we were celebrating."

Ms. Ervin laughed and told Sierra that we were having a celebration and a ceremony and that as soon as everyone was here, we'd begin.

"Oooooh, we having a fashion show, Ms. Ervin. You should've told me. I could've worn my red carpet outfit!" Yesenia was getting excited. "You know I'm a high-fashion model. As soon as I'm sixteen, y'all won't be seeing me in nobody's classroom!"

"Yeah, right," JaVon yelled as he and the rest of the class piled into what used to be our Social Studies classroom. Everyone had something to say about how the room was decorated. Just as the late bell rang, my mom walked in. She smiled and waved at me then walked over to Ms. Ervin.

"Hi, it's been a while. I'm Ms. Simmons, Jasmine's mom.

"Yes, I remember. Good to see you again."

"You too. Thank you so much for doing this."

As soon as my mom finished greeting Ms. Ervin, several adults walked in and introduced themselves. I heard Sekou's dad introduce himself as Brother Kamau. Sekou's mom, Suheir Baruti, came also. Everybody's parents were invited, but only five showed up – mine Sekou's, Sierra's, Alberto's and Yesenia's grandmother. Most of us were leaning against our desks when Ms. Ervin and our parents joined the circle. She instructed us all to stand up then she closed her eyes. The room grew silent without her having to say a word. Sekou's dad spoke first.

"I'm 'Brother Kamau, Sekou's father. I'm going to ask our elder, Sister Rodriguez for permission to begin." He looked at Yesenia's grandmother and she nodded her head yes. Then he said we were going to open our celebration by pouring libations and honoring our ancestors. Ms. Ervin placed a large plant in front of him and he knelt and began what sounded like a prayer. He asked us to listen carefully while he paid homage to our ancestors by speaking their names.

A few of the names, I was familiar with, but the others, I didn't have a clue. He called out, Olaudah Equiano, David

Walker, Araminta Ross, Toussaint L'Ouverture, Telemaque, Denmark Vesey, Ramón Emeterio Betances, Callie House, Martin Delaney, Eugenio María de Hostos, Pedro Albizu Campos, Frederick Douglass, César Chávez, Che Guevara, Sojourner Truth, Ken Saro Wiwa, Stephen Biko, Antonia Pantoja, Queen Nanny, Julia de Burgos, Ella Jo Baker, June Jordan, Constance Baker Motley and Mother Hale. Each time he spoke a name, he poured a little bit of water in the plant.

Then it was our turn to call out names of people we'd learned about this year – the ancestors we wanted to honor. At first, no one said anything. Then we all looked over at Sekou, and he called out "Malcolm X." After that, everyone started calling out the names of Civil Rights leaders like Fannie Lou Hamer, some Black Panthers, Puerto Rican leaders, labors leaders, A. Philip Randolph and Emma Tenayuca, Chicano Rights leaders like Luisa Moreno— a lot of people. I ended by speaking Emmet Till's name, and, as usual, I had to fight back tears when I thought about how he was murdered.

"Right now," Ms. Ervin began, "we're going to take a moment to honor all of those who were enslaved." As she spoke, Mr. Baruti walked behind her desk and took out his djembe. "We want to remember those who survived the Middle Passage, and those who didn't. We want to remember Gus Smith and his family, Jane Simpson and her family.

And all the Africans and their descendants who were held in slavery."

Ms. Ervin paused again, and Sekou's father began softly tapping his drum. Ms. Ervin put her hand over her heart and lowered her voice to a quiet whisper. "I want everyone to close your eyes and put your hand over your heart." She paused and took in a peaceful breath of air. "Now breathe. Slow-ly inhale. Then slow-ly exhale."

She asked us to say a silent prayer for all the men, women, children, grandmothers, grandfathers, healers, doctors, iron workers, master builders, barrel makers, teachers, jelis and scholars who were captured, kidnapped from their homeland and forced into slavery.

I prayed for the grandmother who was forced to eat the chicken. I prayed for all the little children who were born into slavery and for all the women who had their children taken from them. And I thanked God we weren't enslaved any more.

My eyes were still closed when I heard her voice. *Oh my god, it's Dr. Maya Angelou.* Ms. Ervin was playing a recording of Dr. Maya Angelou reciting, *"Still I Rise."* My entire fifth-grade class memorized her poem for our stepping up ceremony. Silently, I spoke the words with her as Sekou's father softly kept the beat with his drum. When I heard Jocelyn and Keyla speaking the words out loud, I did too.

When Dr. Angelou spoke the last line of her poem,

Sekou's father stopped drumming. "Altogether now," he instructed as he beat his drum again, only much louder and a bit faster as we all looked at him and shouted, *"I rise!"* I felt like clapping, but since no one else did, I didn't either.

Ms. Ervin walked to the center of our circle and placed a candle in the middle of the kente cloth that covered a small table. She lit the candle in honor of all of our people who had been enslaved, and she said that, like the smoke from this candle, the spirits of our ancestors had risen. Then she knelt there in silence, for several seconds, as the rest of us stood still. Somber.

"Would anyone like to say anything?"

You could barely hear him. "Thank you," Sekou whispered and looked over at Ms. Ervin. "For teaching us about our ancestors. And I thank our ancestors for all they went through and showing us that if they could get through that, then we can deal with what we have to go through." Ms. Ervin placed her hand over her heart and bowed in Sekou's direction. When no one else spoke, she rose and rejoined the circle.

The longest part of our ceremony was when we took out our pictures and went around the room and talked about our families and what they meant to us. I thanked my mom for coming today, and I said how happy I was that I was going to visit my grandmother who was turning eighty.

A lot of kids said how much they loved their families and

how they couldn't make it without them. Some kids said their mom wanted to come today, but couldn't get off work and to tell Ms. Ervin thank you for having the celebration. A couple of kids didn't want to say anything about their families or their ancestors. And even though we weren't supposed to bring anything, Tiana's mom sent something called *mofongo*. Ms. Ervin said we could take it with us to lunch and Tiana could explain what it was, but only after she got some first.

After we finished, we placed our pictures on the kente cloth so that they surrounded the burning candle. Then, the parents spoke. My mom went first, but she didn't tell me she was going to come to class and put our family on blast. If I had known that, I would have skipped this whole thing. She thanked Ms. Ervin for having this ceremony and for inviting the parents. Then she started talking about dad.

"Mom, stop!" I heard myself say. But when I looked at Sierra who was standing next to me, I realized I'd only spoken those words in my head. *Oh my god, what is she doing?*

"My daughter and I have been through some rough times lately. But Jasmine's father and I used to sing this song to her— any Stevie Wonder fans in the house?" All the parents raised their hands. So did Sekou and a few other kids. I was too paralyzed to raise anything.

"Well, he wrote this beautiful song titled, *Ebony Eyes* and

I want to read, not sing – don't worry Jasmine. But I want to read these lyrics to you. All of you. She paused for a moment. Jasmine's father and I are no longer married, so this may be a bittersweet memory for her, but like Ms. Ervin has been trying to teach you, in order to heal from the past, you have to remember and not run away from the past. Not be ashamed of it."

My mom looked over at me and smiled. You could tell by her face that she knew good and well she shouldn't be doing this. But she was doing it anyway! How is that logical? All I could think when I heard her begin is that this can't really be happening. And although I was still paralyzed, I managed to at least raise my eyebrows in protest! Surely she'll stop now. Nope! She just looked at me and smiled and kept on reading.

I lowered my head and burned a hole in the floor. I couldn't bear to look at everybody looking at me. *It's been a million years since you and dad sang this to me, and now you come here and front like we used to be one big happy family? Apparently we weren't if he decided he had to get the hell out!*

At first, I was seething. But as she continued on about how beautiful I was, how beautiful my eyes were, my heart began to melt. The longer she spoke the words of the song I used to hear at bedtime, the more I wanted to believe her. The more I wanted to be like the girl in the song – the one everybody wanted and wanted to be like. The girl from the ghetto who was BLACK and BEAUTIFUL.

Thank god she was nearing the end of the song I thought as I reminded myself to start breathing again. Wait! Why did she stop?

"Awwwww—"

I raised my head. Keyla was standing there with her hands over her heart.

"—That's so sweet."

I looked over at my mom, and she had tears in her eyes. As she finished speaking the last line of the song, her voice cracked, and everyone started to applaud. When my bottom lip began to tremble, she rushed over and buried me in her arms. "I love you," she whispered as the clapping began to die out. I loved her too, but this was so wrong especially since I was still mad at her. I forced my hands in between her shoulder and my face so I could dry my eyes and at the same time nudge her away. She let me go, but grabbed hold of my hand and squeezed it tight. This time, she didn't let go.

Keyla's mom, Ms. Wilkins's, spoke next.

"This poem that I'm about to read is especially for the young men, but it's for the girls too. I told a co-worker what Ms. Ervin wanted to do today and she said, Levita, you have to read this poem. Then she read it to me and I just shook my head because I think it fits right in with what Ms. Ervin has been trying to teach you. It's written by a friend of hers who lives in D.C., and it's called, "The Highest Bidder.""

A white slaveholder announces:
"Next on the auction block
we have a nigger wench
naked
strong
who can work as long as the day is long
look at her back
and those thighs
along with her hips
sturdy and wide
she is bound to be fertile. . ."

a commercial rapper
raps a rap
about his "skank
ho
bitch
who can make it clap"
now ain't that a switch
instead of the man
an enslaved AfriCAN
make millions
off his lost queen's ass and tits
then justify it
in the name of profits
just business
even define it as progress
yes
profess
that he has advanced the race
because he's keeping pace
with his oppressors
fortune and fame
yet both men inflict pain
and ignore the shameful history

that reduced brothas
to mandingos
that made sistahs
just plain ho's
the auction block is now the concert stage and videos
with rhythmic images of black pimps and voluntary black ho's
she's still naked
while he's dressed in furs and drenched in gold
going once going twice sold
to yield cotton and tobacco for the plantation
going once going twice sold
to keep track number two in heavy rotation
going once going twice sold
for the highest record deal
going once going twice sold
in the name of "keeping it real"
going once going twice sold
to make Forbes's and Fortune's coveted list
going once going twice sold
so deprived niggahs and middle class wiggahs can nod to this
going once going twice sold
in the game playing big pimpin'
going once going twice sold
an unconscious lyricist to an unrighteous system
going once going twice sold
your mama your daughter and your sistah
Going, Going, GONE
BLACK SOULS to the highest bidder

The cheering and clapping was loud enough to be heard from the other end of the hall.

"Yeah!" Jocelyn yelled as she nodded and clapped. "Yeah!"

Other girls were nodding their heads "that's right," too!

"Now we'll hear from Brother Kamau. So, not only is he the father of Sekou and—"

I looked over and saw Ebonee sneaking into our classroom.

"Amaya and Alim," Ms. Baruti said.

"—Amaya and Alim, and the husband of Suheir. He's also, as you've already seen a drummer. On top of all that, he's a brilliant poet and spoken word artist. So, here now with an original piece, Brother Kamau Baruti."

Mr. Baruti stood and took in a deep slow breath. "This piece is dedicated to my queen, my wife, Suheir, and to all the queens in the room. And to all the brothers, young and old. It's dedicated to each of us to remind us of who we really are. And it's called, *Looks Like You.*"

In the beginning was the darkness
Came along long before the light
So how you looking at me covered in midnight
Acting like I ain't right?

Back when anglo saxons saw Africans maxin
We was doing alright until late one hateful night
Open arms welcomed in original sin like long lost kin
But they came armed to fight

Came with an army ordered to harm and smite
Came to replace Orishas with Jesus pieces
Carrying foreign features like those on glass windows
They teach us to stain white

Beat us like animals for being cannibals
While feeding us the flesh and blood of a false Christ
Bitter communion wine drinking white crackers
Jacked us in the middle of the night

Attacked us with savage rachets
Dragged us too far to take flight
Peaceful black magic habits nowhere in sight
Gave us bibles to be the bosses of the resources they swiped

Cavemen wasn't used to sharing fruit so ripe
Recycled our ancient stories into gory allegories
Verses became filled with curses never intended for me
For we pretended the Lord of lords abhors me

When even the Sun shouts: I adore thee
You were made for me as I was for you
The melanin sown in your skin does what its posed to
As every ray reaches you Amen Ra teaches you

Your complexion combines protection with divine direction
No man can erase how it rewinds you
Or the first time it reminds you
Light climbed through space to remind

Your race to shine like stars do
Darkness comes before the dawn when I ignite you
That's why they try to despise you
Tell lies to crucify and confine you

That's why
That's why the night sky reminds you
That's why
That's why the universe looks like you!

By the time he'd reached the end of the poem, Mr. Baruti's eyes were closed as he rocked in the rhythm of his spoken words. "That's why, that's why the night sky reminds you," he said, punctuating each word with confidence. "That's why, that's why the universe looks like you!" We erupted into a thunderous round of applause as Mr. Baruti brought praying hands to his chest and held them there. He bowed as we clapped and clapped and clapped. My head was spinning. But before I had a chance to figure out all he was trying to say, it was like we were at a party on Saturday night.

"Ahhhhhh! No she not playing Rihanna," someone yelled as we all screamed.

"All right! All my queens in the house, say yeah!"

"Yeahhhhh!" We all screamed. Ms. Ervin was getting the party started right.

"Okay ladies. This is your red carpet I-am-a-proud-African-Diasporic-Queen moment!" She was yelling over Rihanna's words and the driving beat. The base commanded us to start bouncing and shaking and popping and locking. "If your ancestors come from Africa, the Dominican Republic, Puerto Rico, Jamaica, Haiti, Cuba, Harlem USA, anywhere in the USA— did I leave anybody out? Then you're an African Diasporic Queen!"

Yesenia was the first to hit the red carpet. Keyla quickly followed. Amber began her red-carpet queen moment and, Dionna, her BFF joined her. Next, Ebonee and I went down together.

"I hope my fellas are getting ready for their red carpet I-am-a-proud-African-Diasporic-Prince moment!"

"Prince? Why we got to be a prince? We Kings!"

"You're kings in training," Ms. Ervin countered. "You've got to show us you're worthy of that title before it's granted to you."

"Ppph! You ain't even a prince yet," Keyla said and shook her butt in JaVon's face."

"You don't just become a king because you call yourself one," Ms. Ervin added.

Before the girls could finish, the guys took to the red carpet and a few of them began dancing all nasty and freaky. Once again, Ms. Ervin put on her you-must-be-on-crack face, then quickly shouted, "JaVon!"

"I'm looking at a lot of kings in training," Sekou's father said as he laughed and shook his head. "Y'all got some work to do, young brothers. Y'all got some work to do."

"Ms. Ervin, Mom, your turn," Keyla shouted.

"Nope! This is your red carpet moment. We'll show you how it's done, old school style in a minute." Ms. Ervin sounded like she really had some moves. "We'll take you back to the original!"

"Oh god, I can't wait to see this," Keyla said as we all continued to dance to Rihanna's *"Don't Stop the Music."*

The entire class was feeling the music and the magic of

the moment as we all danced and sang along with her until the song ended.

"Okay parents, you ready." Ms. Ervin didn't miss a beat as she typed a few keystrokes on the computer.

"Let's show them some old school style. Brother Kamau, Ms. Wilkins, sisters."

Ms. Wilkins covered her mouth and tried to whisper, but we still heard her. "What you playing?"

"Don't worry, we got this," Ms. Ervin said and waved off Ms. Wilkins's fears.

"How old school?" My mom wanted to know.

"Whatever's old school for you."

The next thing you know, this really sexy voice whispered something I couldn't understand. Then the funkiest beat you'd ever want to hear started blaring from the speakers.

"Yeaaahhhh!" We all yelled at the same time, and the whole room started popping and locking since the beat was perfect for that. Ms. Jackson is going to shut this shit down for real, I thought. There was no way not to be freaky on a song like this. You could tell even the parents wanted to get nasty. Sekou's mom and dad started doing some dance they called the bump. Sekou went over and joined them. They looked so cute doing their bump. It looked like a cleaner version of the threesome dances we break out with.

Then, Yesenia and Xiomara started bumping.

"Y'all don't know nothing about the bump," Ms. Ervin yelled and began bumping with Amber's mom.

This joint is hot!" I shouted. This must be where Rihanna got it from, I thought since in *Don't Stop the Music,* she kept repeating the same word over and over just like in this song.

"Ahhhhhhhhhhhhhh!" Everybody was feeling it now!

"All right, keep it clean queens and kings-in-training. Keep it clean!" Ms. Ervin looked dead at JaVon. "Um hmm! You were the one yelling you wanted to be a king!"

"What's that?" We asked when Ms. Wilkins broke out with another cool move.

"Y'all don't know nothing 'bout this!" She yelled. But everything they did, we started imitating 'cause those old school moves were tight!

"Old School! Old School!" We started yelling. "Old School! Old School!"

Not only did this song have the beat and the words, it had this funky saxophone solo, and you could hear cow bells too. And drums, a couple of different kinds of drums. Then a bass guitar kicked in. Then the saxophone again. It's like one-by-one, you got hit with all these funky rhythms. Ms. Ervin started it off— going down the red carpet. Everybody was clapping and smiling and trying their best to show off their moves. I broke out with everything I'd been learning in dance class, and my classmates went wild. "Go Jazz, Go

Jazz, Go Jazz!"

"Jazz got some skills," Derek said and joined me on the red carpet.

The song ended and we all gave ourselves, and the parents, a round of applause.

"Manu Dibango, the first African Musician to ever record a top 40 hit song!" Ms. Ervin was screaming over the applause. "And it got its starts right here in New York City!"

"What's he saying?" Yesenia asked.

"He's from Cameroon, a West African country and makossa is Cameroonian dance music. So makossa means dance— I think," Ms. Ervin said as though she weren't one-hundred percent sure. "So, first Michael sampled his lyrics, now Rihanna. I told you, from Africa, young people, Africa. So much good comes from Africa!"

"Oh my god! I bet you planned this all out," Keyla yelled.

"I bet I did too!" Ms. Ervin said with an attitude. "That's what teachers do!" She smiled and caught her breath. "So, we have a couple of minutes left, it looks like, and we're history. Pun intended!"

"No, Ms. Ervin. Don't leave us!"

"You're leaving me!"

"Hold up! Hold up, everybody." I shook my head convinced JaVon was going to say something half-way stupid. "We really do want to thank you for all you taught us and all you tried to teach us because some of my classmates are a little slow, but give them some time, and they'll catch up— Keyla."

"I'ma smack you!" Keyla raised her hand like she was going to hit JaVon, and Ms. Wilkins pushed it back down, much to JaVon's delight.

I raised my hand. "Thank you for making us think about things differently. I learned so much all year, especially during these past few days," I said then walked over and hugged Ms. Ervin. That set off a chain reaction as the parents moved out of the way so we could all hug her goodbye. And as we hugged our goodbyes, the bell rang.

"Okay young people, out!" Ms. Ervin yelled. Go to lunch!"

"Dag," Yesenia said. "You really not going to miss us."

"I miss you already, but I need to say goodbye to our special guests, and you need to go to lunch."

CHAPTER 9

I left the room, pulled Ebonee next to me and *shhhhed* her. I needed to hear what my mom was going to say and what Ms. Ervin had to say back.

Keyla's mom spoke first. "Ms. Ervin, thank you, thank you, thank you. I asked Keyla what she was reading last weekend 'cause I ain't never seen her read that much. And school is almost over too! So, thank you for all you've done for them. The whole year."

"Yes," I heard a couple of parents say. Maybe it was Yesenia's grandmother and Alberto's mom.

"We had a good year," Ms. Ervin said. "But I don't want it to end here. A lot of them are struggling. Yesterday I sent home a reading list, and I also listed some films that would be good for you to watch with them. They've internalized some really negative stuff, internalized racial inferiority, I call it, and there's all this needing to look a certain way— you know the whole light-skinned, long, straight hair thing, and they have no clue, really, what racism is or how it's impacted them."

"Sister, I read the handout you sent home last weekend, and from what Sekou said, you did an excellent job of helping them understand the whole concept of white supremacy and how it's impacted them."

"No, Brother Kamau, not really, not in five days." Ms. Ervin stopped talking for a second. Knowing her, she was making one of her faces and shaking her head like she'd done a million times this year whenever we tried to argue our point, like she always told us to, but we weren't making any sense.

"Okay, Sister, but what you did do was lay a good foundation—" It was Sekou's dad again.

"So, it's up to you—" Ms. Ervin began.

"That's just what I was thinking." It was Ms. Wilkins. "It's on us now. It's on us."

"—The girls are really struggling," Ms. Ervin continued. "There's such a prejudice, still, against the darker-skinned girls. That on top of everything else they're dealing with at this age."

"It's so true, Ms. Ervin, but it's not just against dark-skinned girls. When I was growing up, we were one of few Hispanic families in the neighborhood, and I used to get beat up all the time, and I never knew why!" That was Ms. Santiago, Sierra's mom. "Sometimes it doesn't pay to look white," she said and laughed like you do when you know you've told a good joke.

"You're right, Ms. Santiago, the prejudices are flying all kinds of ways."

I heard my mom's voice next. "So what do you suggest to help them through this?"

"I'd love to see all our girls *and* boys in some kind of rite of passage program because here, we have to teach academics. Of course we teach other things too, but we can't take the place of a rite of passage program. Our children need that."

"We had that—"

"That's part of our history," Sekou's dad said.

"Absolutely!" Ms. Ervin said. "When we just send them to school, especially these schools, and then let them hang out after school and maybe do a little homework," she hesitated, "we're abandoning them. That may sound harsh, but—"

"You speaking the truth," Ms. Wilkins said.

"—We're just leaving them out there to figure out how to navigate the social and cultural piece on their own and they just can't do it. Or let me put it this way, their way of handling it is gang membership and doing all kinds of ridiculous things to fit in— acting in ways that, deep down, they know are crazy, but if crazy is what they have to do to feel like they matter—" Ms. Ervin paused, "—to their peers? Then crazy it is."

"No Ms. Ervin didn't just call us crazy," I whispered to Ebonee.

"Do you know of any programs like that?" I think that was Tiana's mom.

"Actually, I know some wonderful sisters out in Brooklyn working with our girls. Ms. Simmons, I was actually going to give you their information because I think

Jasmine would benefit greatly from their program. I know she would."

"Yes, I'd love to get their information."

"Me too," Ms. Wilkins said.

"Well, we can't thank you enough for the entire year," Sekou's mom said.

"Yes, thank you. Thank you so much."

That was my cue to be gone. I'd find out more about this rite of passage program soon enough, I thought. Ebonee and I headed for the stairway farthest from Ms. Ervin's door since we didn't want them to know we'd eavesdropped on their conversation.

* * *

The rest of the day flew by, and I couldn't stop thinking about our last class. Ebonee and I couldn't wait to tell our dance teacher about the song we'd heard, *Soul Makossa*, and see if we could create a dance routine for it. This would be our last dance class together for a while since she was going down to North Carolina for half the summer to spend time with her grandmother and her cousins.

Every year, she, her mom and stepdad, and her younger brother and sister would take the train to Burlington. They stayed through the fourth of July and came back, but Ebonee stayed until the end of July. When she got back, we'd spend the rest of the summer dancing in the park, dancing in dance class and going to the movies. This was the first time we'd both be away for the Fourth.

After dance class, Ebonee and I went to her house, ordered a pizza and watched videos. I loved going to her apartment since she had a TV in her room.

After we finished the pizza, we lay on our stomachs and rested our chins in our hands as we watched the video ho's bend and twist. We used to have this running debate on whether the girls in the video had sex with the rappers. She thought they did, because she'd heard some older woman on the subway saying she'd read a book about it.

At first, I didn't believe it. But then I heard some girls arguing in the bathroom, not about whether it was true, but about whether they would or wouldn't do it just to be in the video. Ebonee said they were using the videos to make their way into acting in movies or on TV. She said she could never do that, and she bet most of them regretted it later.

When the second video hit the screen, Ebonee and I locked eyes, and, on cue, jumped off the bed and struck our poses. It was the remix of *Like a Pimp,* and we started bumping and grinding and twisting just like the girls in the video. "Ohhhhhhh," Ebonee moaned as she leaned forward letting her long, shiny hair hang toward the floor. Then she snapped her head up and whipped her hair back. "Ohhhhhhh," she purred as she gyrated from side to side.

"Ohhhhhh," I followed, not to be outdone.

She was the first to fall out laughing. I quickly followed, heaving and gasping as we rolled around on the floor. After we'd exhausted ourselves, we both smoothed back our hair and waited for the next video. "I don't see how they do that for five minutes."

No she didn't just say that. I rolled my eyes at her and dared her to tell another lie. She played dumb.

"Whaaat?"

"August? Lap Dance?"

She waved her hand in the air. "I ain't thinking about Shah. He knows I'm leaving next week and he ain't trying to call nobody. Texting me saying he heard I got a beat down and that's making him look bad."

I just grunted and shook my head.

"Ahhhhhh!" Ebonee was on her feet again, bumping and grinding. "Ms. Ervin shoulda played this today," she said and began singing along with David Banner on his song, *Get Like Me*.

"Chris Brown is the best part of this video!" I was already salivating.

"I know, right."

How could anyone disagree? "Oooh, oooh! Here he comes, here he comes," I yelled, transfixed by the sight of him in his white T-shirt, red baseball cap and his absolutely perfect caramel skin. He was too fine!

We continued to sing along until the white girl showed

up. "Why he gotta be with a white girl?" I yelled as I slapped at the TV.

"She's not white."

"Yes she is!"

"Which one?" Ebonee stopped dancing long enough to see who I was talking about. "Oh," she said like she was surprised."

I pointed my finger in her face as I sang along. She was the one who needed to get another man, just like the song said. The camera panned back over to the white girl with the long, jet black hair. This time, I ignored her and focused on Chris Brown.

"Actually—" Ebonee began, "—she looks more Spanish to me. Like maybe she's from Columbia or something. Like Shakira."

"Yeah, but why she got to be the first one he gets all up on?"

"Stop hatin', Jazz. He has all types of girls in there."

"No."

"Yes."

"Noooooo." I was all up in Ebonee's face now!

"Don't even try it," she yelled and simultaneously pushed me away. "There are dark-skinned girls there."

"She's not dark-skinned. Her skin is brown, and the only reason she's even there is because she has a big butt and size triple-Ds!" Ebonee threw up her hands, waved me off and kept on dancing. "That's all boys care about," I yelled over the music. "Body parts!"

As soon as the video ended, Ebonee wanted to know if I thought Shaheem would really cheat on her when she was in North Carolina. I told her she would know better than I would. Then she asked me if I was going to spend time with my dad in South Carolina. But just like she didn't want to talk about light-skinned girls, I didn't want to talk about my father.

It was almost 9:30 when I got home. My mom was on the phone telling Aunt Angie about Ms. Ervin's class. She'd made some veggie lasagna, and she'd left a note reminding me to put it away when I was done. I fixed myself a plate and took it to my room. Then I turned on my computer and live streamed my favorite radio station. A few seconds later, mom was knocking on my door.

"Congratulations!"

I smiled. Not because I thought it was a big deal to graduate from the eighth grade, but because I was happy to be leaving middle school. I hoped things would get better in high school, but all I could do was wait and see.

"So, that celebration was beautiful!"

"I liked the poem Ms. Wilkins read. And the song too," I said and looked over at her. "Not at first. But thanks."

"I actually didn't go back to work afterward," she said as she sat down on the bed next to me. "I kept thinking about what you asked me the other night— about your father." I waited for her to continue. "He probably did marry me because I'm light . . . And because he loved me."

She grabbed my hand and made me look her in the eyes. "I know you want boys to like you. But when I was in high school, it wasn't easy being the girl, or one of the girls, that everybody wanted. There was a time when I felt like all I was good for was to be somebody's girlfriend, and, deep down, I knew I was so much more than my looks. But it didn't matter 'cause I got it from both sides. I got attention from the boys, but the girls hated me because they thought I was stuck up." My mom threw her head back and laughed.

"Why is that funny?"

"I wasn't stuck up," she said, still laughing. "I was terrified."

"Of what?"

She took a deep breath in. "So, I started to believe the hype. Then, I didn't know who I was. Didn't know if I was just another pretty face or what. I always got good grades, so I knew I was smart, but boys weren't asking me out because I was smart. Only one thing mattered to them." She sighed and slowly moved her head right to left. "I was all messed up," she said finally.

I couldn't believe I was hearing this. Did Ebonee feel this way?

"Now, I'm working for a dark-skinned supervisor who

can't stand me because I'm light-skinned!" My mom just stared at me. Aunt Angie said she was having a rough time at work, but I didn't know she meant this. I didn't know what to say.

"Jasmine, I don't want you growing up all confused like I was. Life is hard enough without having to worry about your own people hating you because of your color."

"But people do hate on dark-skinned people."

"I know they do."

"Ms. Ervin said this started from slavery. From White people."

"And now we running around here terrorizing each other with this mess."

It's not like anybody Spanish or White would marry Your Black Ass!

Shut up! I yelled to the evil voice inside my head. *I'm sick of you!*

"I spoke with your father. I called him today to make sure he knew we'd be there Saturday. He said he was looking forward to seeing you and Dalani. I also—"

"What?" I glared at her.

"He's looking forward to seeing you—"

"I heard you!" My breathing grew quicker and angrier. I could feel a fire smoldering in my stomach. "I'm not looking forward to seeing him. You know that's f____d up." My mom cut her eyes at me. I'd cursed in front of her one time before but never again. Until now.

"Jasmine, you need to," she held up her hand as if doing so stopped her from finishing her sentence. "I can't explain why your fa—"

"Did I ask you to explain anything!" My mom looked me dead in the eye, and she got up, and she left my room. I watched her leave as I simultaneously burned a hole through her back. Even though she had never hit me before, just now, she looked like she wanted to slap me into next Wednesday.

I can't stand you! Or my f____g color struck father. With your ignorant ass. . . Saying you want to see me when you've haven't seen me in almost a year. . .

I'm a baby still
Please, nurture me with bold love
so I can stand tall

CHAPTER 10

My mom and I barely spoke to each other all weekend. We didn't revisit the subject of my dad until late Monday morning when we were on our way to the airport. She told me she understood why I was angry. She said she wanted me to enjoy my time with Mama Roxie. She said I probably wouldn't see my father until Saturday, at the party, and she knew *everyone* would have a great time. I heard everything she said. I also heard everything she didn't say. Loud and clear.

I couldn't stop thinking about what she'd said about being in high school. I wondered if Ebonee ever got freaked out by all the attention she got. When we reached the airport, my mom waited with me until it was time to board the plane. Then, she told me how much she loved me, and she hugged me like she hadn't in a long time. The minute I was out of her sight, I broke down. When I got on the plane and took my seat, the flight attendant asked me if I was okay. I told her my aunt had just died and the funeral was yesterday, but that I'd be okay. She said she was sorry and that she'd come back to check on me.

This was my second time flying and my first time flying alone. I was beginning to feel like I'd been alone all my life. *My color struck father is MIA. My mom thinks dark-skinned people are the ones with the problem, just because she has a hater at work. What about what she's been through all her life? Maybe she has a reason to hate. I bet you never thought about that. And Ebonee's in her own little mixed up world. All she cares about is herself.*

Thank God she bought me an iPod for being her "brilliant soon-to-be high-schooler." And also because she loves me. Yeah right, I thought. Still, it couldn't have come at a better time.

My plane landed safely, and my uncle Earl picked me up from the Charleston airport. I had met all of my aunts on my dad's side when we went to D.C. for our family reunion, but not all of my uncles. I vaguely remembered Uncle Earl, but it wouldn't have matter if I hadn't since he looked just my father. Mama Roxie had ten children in all, and my father was the youngest.

As we headed for Johns Island, Uncle Earl acted like a tour guide giving me the history of the Low Country. People called the area near this part of South Carolina's coast the Low Country, my uncle said, because it's at sea level and flat. At first, the area looked like a regular city. As we headed out of Charleston though, we came upon the first of several bridges I would cross during my stay there.

The bridges connected the Sea Islands to Charleston and to each other. The saltwater smell was as strong as the sun was hot. I'd never smelled salt water in the air before, nor had I ever seen marshes. It was eighty-eight degrees, and my uncle told me to get ready for a hot South Carolina week.

As we drove further, I saw palm trees. Really? In South Carolina? "I thought palm trees were only in L.A.?"

"Nope," Uncle Earl informed me. "The Sabal Palmetto tree," its official name, "is South Carolina's state tree." He said that Florida also claimed the palm tree as its state tree, but that it was South Carolina's state symbol and that made South Carolina, not Florida, the palm tree capital of the world. New York is the Maple Tree state I thought but didn't bother to say out loud.

As we approached the second bridge, the Stono Bridge, he called it, my heart beat faster and my body stiffened. We'd driven over a huge bridge when we went to DC, and it wasn't my favorite part of the trip then either. Whenever we came to a bridge, I always had these crazy thoughts that we were going to somehow go over the side and fall into the water. I didn't mind being up high in a plane, but whenever I crossed a high bridge, I was terrified.

The Stono Bridge crossed the Stono River where a slave rebellion had taken place further down in St. Paul's Parish, Uncle Earl said. Fifty to one-hundred enslaved men had gotten guns and tried to escape to Florida, but they were no match for the White men who hunted them down and killed them, he said. Before they were killed, though, they marched more than ten miles and killed between twenty and twenty-five White people.

Good, I thought.

But after that, he said, the town passed the Negro Act limiting the Africans' privileges. They would no longer be allowed to earn what little bit of money some were able to earn or grow their own food or get together to sing and dance on their day off. I can't believe this, I thought. School is over! I'm not trying to spend my summer vacation hearing about slavery in South Carolina. And I'm definitely not trying to visit places where our ancestors had been murdered.

As soon as we crossed the Stono Bridge, my uncle said we had left James Island and were now on Johns Island. We'd started out in Charleston and, in forty minutes, we were on our second island. But where was the beach, I wondered. And why did this island look like any other city? I thought an island would look like— an island! The palm trees were different, though, and I still couldn't believe how many there were. There were a lot of trees period. The others were oak trees, Live Oak trees, Uncle Earl said, and they were everywhere.

After driving past a gas station, the post office, a CVS store, a grocery store and several other retail shops, we turned onto this two-lane road. There were a few businesses on this road, but there were far more trees. The more we drove, the more it looked like a scene from the Wizard of Oz since the trees lined the both sides of the roadway. The long, tentacle-like branches stretched out horizontally across the two-lane road, and at any minute, I was expecting them to reach down, wind around our car like a snake then lift us in the air. Who knew what would happen then. Maybe they'd keep us trapped as we screamed for our lives or twirl us around until we got car sick and passed out.

At night it must be really spooky, I thought. Even now it was weird. I kept wondering how the branches could stretch out like that and not break. What happened when it snowed? Weren't they afraid of the branches getting too heavy and crashing down on their cars?

In New York, they'd carve most of these branches off. It must not snow much down here, I thought. I'd never been to a rainforest, but this must be what a rainforest looks like since the cover of the branches shielded us from the sun. As we drove, it looked as though a light was flashing down on us, except instead of a light, it was the sun peeking in through the branches that didn't provide complete shade.

Even more weird, though was what was hanging from the branches. It looked just like tinsel hanging from a Christmas tree except, instead of being shiny, it was a dull grey. My uncle told me it was Spanish Moss. He said the Indians called it "tree hair," and they used it to stuff their mattresses. He said it's still used to stuff mattress and also some seat cushions. Johns Island definitely didn't look like a regular city now. But where is the beach?

I never saw the beach, but, the more we drove, the more really nice houses we passed. Then we came upon some dirty, run down trailers. Oh my god, Mama Roxie doesn't live in a trailer, does she? This really is the country now, I thought. We turned left onto another two-lane road and I began to see houses again. But they were so far apart, I wondered if the people knew each other. When my uncle turned left onto a dirt road, he announced that we were almost home. This is OD, I thought! You just turned into the woods and you're telling me we're almost home? Who does he think I am Little Red Riding Hood? All there was was woods. Until we came upon a house set way back from the unpaved road.

"That's your Aunt Angeline's house," Uncle Earl said. "You remember her?"

I didn't know if I remembered her or not, but I said I did anyway.

We passed by another house on the opposite side of the road and my uncle began to slow down. About fifty yards later, we pulled into the driveway of a nice white wood-framed house, and I saw Mama Roxie sitting on the porch in her rocking chair. I got out of the car and walked excitedly to the porch.

"Look at you!" She reached down, grabbed my shoulders and kissed me on the face. I don't think anyone kissed harder than my grandma.

"I missed you, Grandma."

"Baby, I speak to you and your brother every day. Your

picture sits right on my nightstand. You and Dalani and all my grands. Are you hungry?"

"Yes."

"Come on in here!" She had the widest smile on her face.

Uncle Earl got my suitcase out of the trunk and brought it in the house. He told Mama Roxie to call him when she needed to go shopping, then he left.

"Now I know your mama is a vegetarian, but what do you eat?"

"Not me, I eat meat."

"That's what she said, but I thought I'd ask. I know mothers and daughters don't always agree on things," she said and smiled.

Mama Roxie went into the refrigerator and pulled out a salad with lettuce and tomatoes and cucumbers that she'd picked from her garden. She boiled some sweet yellow corn, also from her garden, and warmed some baked chicken from the night before. After we ate, she went into her closet and pulled out two sun hats – one for her and one for me. "Look at you! Your skin is so dark and pretty," she said and smiled. "And don't you ever stop smiling. Your smile is almost as bright as the sun! Has anybody ever told you that?"

"No."

"Well are you smiling? Because if anyone's ever seen your smile, then I know they would've told you how beautiful it is."

"Thank you," I said and smiled even wider. The sun hat that she'd given me was too big. It felt like any minute it would fall off my head. "Mama Roxie, I think it's too big."

"Pull the string," she instructed. "There," she said and nodded her head after I'd tightened it.

We walked out to the front yard to her vegetable garden. She reached inside a bucket and pulled out two pairs of gloves. After we'd put our gloves on, Mama Roxie gathered up her dress then sat down in the dirt. Okay, I thought. I know she's not expecting me to sit in the dirt. And do what? I wondered.

"Come on down here, Jasmine, and I'll teach you how to pull up weeds by the roots."

Umm, doesn't she see I'm wearing shorts, I thought to myself as I did exactly as I was told.

"Have you ever worked in a garden before, Jasmine?"

"No mam."

"Well you are in for a treat! Most days, I can get down here and get back up on my own. But I'm glad you're here just in case Grandma needs some help getting up," she said and smiled. She had lost some weight since the last time I saw her, so I figured I was strong enough to pull her up if she needed me to.

"Now, these weeds come into my garden and try to take all the nourishment away from my tomatoes and my squash and all my other vegetables. Just greedy, greedy," she said as she made a Grinch face and shook her head. Then she smiled. Mama Roxie had the cutest smile, and a cute little gap between her front teeth. She reminded me of a really cute chipmunk when she smiled. And she didn't have any wrinkles, except on her forehead when she frowned. How could she be almost eighty and no wrinkles, I wondered.

"So, you and I are going to remove them so my plants get everything they need to grow." She showed me how to dig my fingers into the dirt, pinch my thumb and index finger together and pull the weeds up by the root. "That's it," she said when I successfully conquered my first one. "You know, there are some people who are just like weeds."

For a long while, neither of us talked. She did begin to hum though, and sing too. We worked and she sang. I heard other sounds also — insects buzzing and occasionally, beautiful, clear notes from the wind chime hanging from one of the trees. Other than her singing, the insects and the wind chime, it was really quiet. And still.

"You tired?"

"I'm okay," I said.

"You know, when your father was a boy, he used to love to play in the dirt," she began. "I never had to tell him twice to come help me weed because he just loved to be in the dirt. Now his sister, Angeline, she was just like him, a tomboy really. But my sister — my cousin really, but we were raised like sisters — Annie Mae, just couldn't stand dark children."

Mama Roxie stopped weeding, lifted her head and looked over at me. "Can you imagine that? All her children were all brown-skinned except for one who was light. But my children were dark-skinned, and she used to yell to Angeline, 'girl don't play in the sun.' One time I caught your father calling her a tar baby." Mama Roxie stopped talking.

"What did you do?"

"I tore his behind up! My youngest child. And I knew where he got it from, but it didn't matter. This is your blood, I told him, and God made us all Black and beautiful." Grandma and I continued with our weeding as the sun bore down. She had on a long indigo cotton dress that covered her legs. I had on a T-shirt and some shorts, but I'd begun to wish I'd worn a dress.

"One Summer, I was called away by the Pardoos. Gone for a week straight, tending to their house and their children. So my youngest ones, Angeline, your Uncle Earl, Elijah and your father, went to stay with Annie Lee. Your father and Elijah were still in diapers. When Earl told me that Annie Lee made Angeline sleep on the porch for the first two nights—" she paused and shook her head like she was trying to shake loose a bad memory. "Well, that's in the past."

"Grandma, how come— I mean, why was she like that?"
"Jasmine, some of us have been confused ever since slavery ended. To hear the old folks tell it, some were confused

before it ended. Really, they were scared is what they were. They were just trying to survive and over time, they got more and more sick. Not sick with a fever or pneumonia, but with something much worse. This was the sickness the White people gave us. And it seems like we got that sickness just as bad today as ever."

She could tell I didn't get what she was saying.

"A lot of us back then, and even today, mistook not being a slave as the same thing as being free. Now, most slaves got their emancipation and ended up sharecropping, which meant they were still slaves but now they had to pay for their own housing and food. Some were lucky and got some land. Some of the free Africans and Blacks already had land. But what I know is that if you don't have any land or something you own, then you're not really free. Your spirit might be free, but as far as money goes, you're still trapped."

We just learned about this in Social Studies, I thought.

"So, this one had land and was able to work hard and make a living and pass the land down to their children and that one had his family, a change of clothes, a pair of shoes and a strong back."

"So the Black people with land thought they were better than the Black people who didn't have land?"

"They thought they were closer to White is what they thought," she said, then added, "Some, not all. Folks used to say it was like the nearer to White you were, the more White folks respected you. And if you had the White folks on your side, life might be a little easier. Now, some of the lighter-skinned ones looked like they could've been White and when they were able to acquire property and build churches and what have you, if that sickness took hold and you were dark-skinned, you weren't welcomed. Even though they were free and had some land and more money than the rest of, they were still slaves in their spirits."

"My Social Studies teacher said that wealth was passed down to White people, even the ones who didn't own slaves, and poverty was passed to Black people, and that they got a head start.

"That's right."

"She said we're ashamed because we were enslaved and some people are ashamed because they're poor."

"Jasmine, those people who were set free had spent all that time during slavery being treated as if they were nothing. Property!" She shook her head from side to side. "They needed a healing is what they needed, but it never happened." She paused for a moment. "We have spent so much time being ashamed of our history, and we try to escape it by acquiring things. But even when you acquire things, you're still not as good as White folks, in their eyes," she said and laughed. "But you know what the real shame is, Jasmine?" Mama Roxie was no longer smiling, and the pain on her face scared me. "Not knowing your own goodness no matter what anyone else thinks. That's the real shame."

After we finished weeding, Mama Roxie showed me how to turn a bed which means she showed me how to dig up a row of dirt that she was going to plant more seeds in.

Afterward, we went inside to get cleaned up and Mama Roxie made dinner while I watched TV. Whenever she was in the kitchen, she either sang or hummed, church songs mostly.

We spent the next three days cooking, working in the garden and canning beans, tomatoes and peaches. She loved peaches. I even went with her into the chicken coop to gather freshly laid eggs. The best time though was the night she showed me how to cook her famous rolls. No one's rolls tasted better than Mama Roxie's. Before my mom and dad separated, Mama Roxie stayed with us during the summer, and she would always bake her rolls.

"Do y'all have rolls like this in restaurants in Harlem," she asked me knowing good and well nobody made rolls as good as she did."

"Grandma, are you serious? You know nobody can make these like you." Her smile said it all. She just wanted me to brag about how good they tasted! "Do you like it better here than in Harlem?" I asked her.

"Chile yes! In Harlem, I could never feel the way I do here. Here I got my vegetable garden, my flower garden, all my animals."

"Your animals?"

"Yes! The birds that wake me up every day and the chickens and roosters that help them. The rabbits that just love to run through my yard and think they gonna eat my lettuce. The crickets that sing when night falls." She looked at me and smiled. "You'll hear them tonight. Then there's the old garden snakes that wind their way around every now and then. And the most beautiful butterflies that come and just sit on my flowers.

"Butterflies are such a blessing." She looked just like the Grinch did when he found out the real meaning of Christmas. "Such a blessing! You mark my words, tomorrow, mid-morning, the most beautiful Eastern Tiger Swallowtail will stop by to greet you. I told her my grandbaby from Harlem was coming to visit."

"How does it look?" I asked.

"You'll know it when you see it. If she likes you, she'll fly close enough for you to see her orange and blue spots."

Wait 'til I text Ebonee and tell her my granny is a butterfly whisperer, I thought and half-smiled.

Mama Roxie and I ate dinner then cleaned up the kitchen. Afterward, she invited me to sit with her on the porch and watch the sunset. I couldn't believe how quiet it was out here. I guess if you live in the woods, it should be quiet. But this was beyond quiet. It felt as though time had stopped and you were just— here. It was weird at first, but then I got used to it. I don't know why, but it made me feel calm. It was weird to feel calm.

A little later, we went to see how high the rolls had risen. She said that in the morning, they'd be ready to go into the oven and we'd have fresh rolls for breakfast. Even though it was only nine thirty, I was sleepy and ready for bed. Gardening makes you tired, I thought.

I was in the bathroom brushing my teeth when I saw it. In the tub. It was like a cross between a daddy long legs and some kind of black ugly bug that hopped around like a frog. The biggest bug I'd ever seen. I took off my slipper, took aim and hurled it at the bug. It was too quick. It hopped out of the way. Damn! I thought. I have to smash it. Then the bottom of my slipper will be nasty and I'll have to wipe it off. The thought of it made me cringe. Oh well, I said to myself. There was no way this bug was staying in the house with us. "Okay," I whispered as I leaned against the tub and took aim. For a split second, I held my breath—

"Whaaaaccckkk!

"Yuck," I said as I pulled my slipper away. I turned on the cold water and ran it over my slipper. Once most of the bug had disappeared, I used toilet paper to remove the rest.

"Jasmine, you all right?"

"Yes mam." I tied a scarf around my head, turned off the light and went into Grandma's bedroom.

"You ready for bed?"

"Yes mam. I killed this big bug in the bathtub." Her eyes widened in fear, and so did mine. "You killed Peter!" She looked like she was going to cry, and her voice had changed to a much higher pitch. So had mine.

"I'm sorry, Grandma."

"It's okay, baby," she said, quickly regaining her composure.

"Grandma, I'm sorry. I didn't know I wasn't supposed to kill it. I'm sorry grand—"

"It's all right," she said in hushed tones and shook her head sideways. Then she walked over to me and hugged me tight. As she loosened her grip, she kissed me on the forehead.

"He was one of your pets?" I asked looking up at her.

Mama Roxie closed her eyes. "Jasmine, clear your mind before you lay down. And before you close your eyes, always thank God for all of today's blessings so that when you wake up tomorrow morning, you'll be ready to receive tomorrow's blessings." She said the same thing every night before I went to bed. I hugged her and told her goodnight.

"Goodnight, baby."

I closed the door to my bedroom and grabbed my Sidekick. I opened it and began texting: *Hey! Having mad fun! My grndmthr luvs bugs. Killed huge bug in bathtub. His name was Peter. How was I posed to know he was her pet? I'm Sure she 4givs u. NC is fun. Big celebr8tion Fri. Met a cute boy.*

*Chilaun. Cool name, right! Luvs bsktball n me! Shaheem said
he missed me. LOL!*

I told her that I thought my grandmother would forgive
me, and I told her about all the trees and how spooky it was
driving to Mama Roxie's house. I also went on about how
great my grandmother's rolls were. She told me she'd text me
a picture of her and Chilaun while they were at the
amusement park. I closed my eyes as the crickets, and some
frogs too, sang me to sleep.

CHAPTER 11

The first time I heard a rooster crow was one morning when Ebonee and I got lost in the Bronx. We were looking for a community center and ended up at this huge garden run by a cool man named Talib. If we hadn't heard the rooster crowing, we would've walked right past it since we weren't expecting to see a garden, a farm almost, in the middle of New York. Mama Roxie had already starting cooking breakfast when the rooster crowed this morning.

"Hi Grandma."

"Good morning. And how are you?" She asked as she stood at the kitchen sink.

"Good."

"Did you sleep well?"

"Yes mam."

"Are you ready for today's blessings?"

"I'm ready for some rolls," I said and smiled. She cut her eyes at me then returned my smile. "Yes mam."

"So to finish them off, I take this brush and dip it in this melted butter—" She paused and I watched as she carefully brushed the rolls with the liquid butter. Cooking and baking were definitely her things. And gardening and watching her pets and singing and sitting on the porch. I can see why she liked it better down here. She wouldn't be able to do half that in New York.

"—So when they come out, they'll be nice and brown on

top," she said as she picked them up and put them in the oven. "Do they teach cooking in school nowadays?"

"Some schools you can go to and they specialize in culinary arts, but I'm going to a regular high school next year. I'll be in the honors program though."

"How was school this year?"

"It was all right. I'm glad I'm in high school now. They say its better."

"Better than what?"

"Than middle school. People are more mature. Not as childish or mean, I guess."

"Are the children still getting strung out on drugs?"

"No. Not in middle school anyway."

"You're not caught up in drugs are you?"

"No mam."

"Good. I watched drugs destroy just about the whole community when I lived in Harlem. Before you were born. It was a shame."

"You have so many trees here," I said as I looked out the kitchen window.

"Yes, Live Oak trees," she said and nodded her head. "Except the little baby growing over there. You see it there?"

"Uh huh."

"That's a Pin Oak. We planted that last year."

"Who?"

"Me and Sister Muhsinah, my angel."

"Who is Sister Muhsinah?"

"She'll be here Friday. She wants to meet both you and Dalani. She used to be a reporter, but now she's a teacher."

"Why is she your angel?"

"She and I became friends a while back when she was still a reporter. She visits me and we sit and talk and have meals together. During the summer, she helps me in my garden. She and your uncle Elijah. I couldn't keep it up without their help. Earl does all the heavy lifting work and Muhsinah helps with planting and weeding and anything else it needs."

"Why did you plant another tree, Mama Roxie?"

"Do you remember what happened last year in Jena, Louisiana?" I shook my head no. "You don't remember when they put the Black children in jail after they fought some of the White kids because the White kids had hung a noose on the tree at the school after the Black kids sat under the tree?"

"Oh yeah! The Jena Six."

"'The White tree,' they called it, like it was only for White kids! God ain't made no White tree!" Mama Roxie was getting angry. "God ain't made no Black tree! God blesses us with trees," she said and shook her head in disgust. "So, you know all the leaders went down there and marched and they told us to wear black. I never wear black, except for a funeral, but I shore wore black that day. And, Jasmine, do you remember what the people at the school did after all the fighting started?" I shook my head no. "We didn't find out until later." Mama Roxie stopped talking as if what she was about to say was too painful. "They cut down that tree." Her voice was much lower now. "I cried when I heard that. Can you imagine cutting down a tree? Umm!"

Her whole body shook like she'd just gotten a chill. She leaned against the sink, closed her eyes and started to sing. "Sometimes I feel discouraged. And think my work's in vain. But then the Holy Spirit. Revives my soul again." Her voice was booming now, and I could feel the vibration from the sounds coming out of her mouth. "There is a balm. In Gilead. To make the wounded whole. There is a balm. In Gilead. To heal the sin sick soul." She slammed her hands together in one loud clap then walked over to the table and sat down.

"I didn't know they cut the tree down," I said hoping she could see how sorry I was that it made her so sad."

"Do you know how sacred a tree is, Jasmine?" I just looked at her. "Did cutting down that tree solve anything?" She asked me.

"No mam," I said and looked out the window. "The tree they cut down was a Pin Oak tree?"

"Yes. Muhsinah called the school for me to find out, and they said it was a Pin Oak tree. So we dug and we planted us a Pin Oak tree right out there. We said a prayer for the Pin Oak tree that was cut down and for the fools who cut it down. And we said a prayer for the children and their parents, and for all the children everywhere."

Silence filled the space between us, and I wondered what things were like at that high school now. There were very few white kids in my elementary school. None really. None in my middle school either. I wondered if anyone else was as upset as Grandma that they cut the tree down.

"Jasmine, you can't cut out hatred. Just like the doctors who try to cut cancer out of someone's body— it can't be done. You have to heal at the root! And that tree was not the root of the problem. That tree was not the problem at all. I still get angry when I think about it." Mama Roxie looked at the clock. The smell of the rolls had activated my saliva glands.

"The rolls smell so good," I said.

"Look in the cabinet and get two plates and set the table, please."

"Yes mam."

"The forks are in the drawer next to the refrigerator." Mama Roxie got up to take the rolls out of the oven. "So, baby, whenever there's a hurt in your soul, that's not the time to start cutting things out or taking drugs or trying to change how you look. That's the time to go back to your roots 'cause your roots will sustain you," she said and paused. "Have you ever seen a tree without roots?" I shook my head no. "I know you haven't 'cause it doesn't exist. Do you know what the roots do for the tree?"

"Don't they feed it?" I asked knowing I was right.

"Yes. The roots feed the tree the water and the nutrients it needs to grow, and they anchor the tree to the ground so it can stand strong and tall." She should have been a science teacher, I thought. "Jasmine, when a tree is cut off from its roots, it dies."

"Our social studies teacher, Ms. Ervin taught us about our African roots."

"What did she teach you?"

"That the Africans who were forced into slavery were human beings and many were under twenty years old."

"What else?"

"She also told us about enslaved Africans who were healers. That's right, one man was from South Carolina."

"Sampson," she said. "He cured snake bites better than anyone else."

"Yeah." I was amazed. "Mama Roxie how did you know?"

"You think because your grandmother didn't go to college she ain't intelligent?"

"No mam."

"Yup, the governor freed Sampson and gave him one-hundred dollars a year for life. But Sampson was already free in his spirit. Free enough to know not to let go of what he brought over with him from Africa."

"You learned about him in school, too?"

"Baby, no. What did you say, Ms. Ervin taught you about your African roots? Well my mother, your great-grandmother, taught us about our roots. She was a healer, you know. You come from a long line of healers. Your daddy's a healer— a wounded healer, but a healer nonetheless. And he married a healer. Jasmine, what do you think happens to people who don't know their roots? Where they come from and who their people are?"

"They're confused, I guess."

"Confused, angry and don't know why. All messed up."

"But I didn't really want to know about my roots until Ms. Ervin taught us to look at slavery from a different perspective."

"Baby, your roots don't begin in slavery," she said and looked me in the eye. "They begin in Africa, where our people come from. And when they came over here, they didn't forget their roots. They didn't try to cure no sickness with no knife. They used herbs and they used the fire in their spirits. They used the love God gave 'em so whoever was sick could heal from the inside. You can't heal from the outside without healing from the inside."

"But it's hard not to be ashamed of where you came from if you think it's bad."

"I know, baby. But remember, a tree cut off from its roots is a dead tree. And whatever bad there may be, there's always a lot more good. Bad don't cancel out good! And we've got to celebrate the good. We've got to heal from this sickness that's been passed on to us, thinking White folk are better because they think it themselves! Trying to be like them!" Mama Roxie took my hand in hers and reassured me with her eyes. "We can't be ashamed of our dark skin, Jasmine. We've got to love who we are. We've got to love how we look 'cause God didn't make no mistakes."

Tell that to the boys who make fun of dark-skinned girls. And the girls who look down on them.

"Have you ever looked at the night sky with all those white stars and a beautiful moon?"

"Yes."

"What else did you see, besides the moon and the stars?"

"The sky, I guess."

"What color is the sky?"

"It's black."

"Uh huh!"

"Black like me," I said in a whisper.

"It's beautiful. Beautiful like you, Jasmine. Beautiful like you."

It was as though Mama Roxie knew everything we'd studied last week in school and she was making it a point to review it with me. Mom must've told her everything. Or maybe she'd heard Sekou's father poem, I thought and laughed inside. The poem that said we were loved by God, no matter who said otherwise. "That's why, that's why the night sky reminds you." I rolled the words around in my head like a spoken word artist. "That's why, that's why the universe looks like you!"

We sat down to eat, and Mama Roxie asked me to say the blessing. After breakfast, complete with fresh eggs Mama Roxie had gathered that morning, we cleaned up the kitchen and took out the trash. Mama Roxie said I didn't have to work in the garden this morning if I didn't want to, but that she'd miss me since I was an excellent gardener and great company. I went into my room to put on my gardening clothes. I thought about Ebonee, and I wondered what she was doing. I wished she were here so we could talk about everything Mama Roxie and I had been talking about.

After getting dressed, I picked up my journal and went outside. I sat down in the rocking chair and waited to see if any of Grandma's pets would come around. I knew now to let everything live, no matter how creepy it was. If I saw a snake though, I was locking myself in the house forever.

No sooner than when I opened my journal and turned the page, the most beautiful butterfly came fluttering by. It was yellow and black, like a tiger. It settled on some flowers that lined the walkway, and I saw them! The blue and orange spots on the inside tips of its wings. Wow! She said it would come and visit me.

I felt like I did last year on my birthday when my dad promised to take me to BBQs, and he actually showed up.

Mama Roxie said she was going to come and welcome me, and she did! I wondered what she'd named it. I looked at all the trees surrounding her house. I thought about them cutting down the tree at the high school in Jena and about the Billie Holiday song Ms. Ervin played when we studied the music of the Jim Crow era. I watched the squirrels running along the branches of the tree, and I picked up my pen and I began to write.

> *Regal Live Oak trees*
> *Acorns and squirrels on branches*
> *That once bore strange fruit*

Blood on the leaves, blood at the root. Poplar trees bear strange fruit. I could hear that song in my head even though we'd only heard it a couple of times. I could hear Mama Roxie's voice too. *But the blood didn't come from the tree. It was evil that brought the blood to the tree and to the root. See what I mean, baby. Ain't nothing wrong with the tree!* I never knew she was so smart. She moved back to South Carolina a year before I was born, but she stayed with us during the summer whenever my Uncle Elijah drove her to New York. I wondered why she moved to New York to begin with.

"Jasmine," she yelled.

"Yes mam?"

"Bring me the large aluminum bowl please."

"Okay."

We gardened until ten that morning. She said Uncle Earl would be here soon to take us into town. Before he came, I asked her, why she moved to New York. She stopped digging and looked over at me. "Well, in 1966, our house burned to the ground. We didn't have any insurance, so your grandfather and I went up north to stay with his brother and his family."

"How old was my father?"

"Let me see, Calvin was," she squinted her eyes, "Six, I believe. Yes, six. But I left him, Elijah, Angeline and Earl here to stay with their grandmother, and the others came with us. Your grandfather's brother, Willie had left about ten years earlier, and he'd been trying to get me and Horace to come up there."

"Why did Horace, I mean his brother, come?"

"Jasmine—" Mama Roxie slowly shook her head. "—a lot of us had to get outta here quick. It wasn't safe for Black people back then. Especially those who worked for the NAACP on voter registration."

"Did you work in the NAACP?"

"Do you know who Septima Clark is?"

"No mam."

"You know who Dr. Martin Luther King Jr. is?"

"Of course."

"And you know who Rosa Parks is?"

"Yes."

"Mrs. Clark taught Mrs. Parks. Mrs. Parks said Septima Clark inspired her and gave her the courage to sit down and not get up. It's a shame school children know who Rosa Parks and Dr. King are, but y'all don't Septima Clark."

"We never studied her."

"When Dr. King was awarded the Nobel Peace Prize in 1965, who do you think went with him to receive his honor?" I shrugged my shoulders. "Septima Clark! Dr. King insisted that she go with him. He said she deserved just as much credit for what was happening in the movement as he did."

"Seriously?"

"I went to Mrs. Clark's Citizenship School here on Johns Island. She got fired from her teaching job because she refused to quit the NAACP like they told her to," Mama Roxie said and paused. "But a lot of folk got much worse than that. Much worse. Mrs. Clark trained Esau Jenkins who opened up the first Citizenship School on Johns Island. And I was taught by Mr. Jenkins."

"What is a Citizenship School? And what happened after she was fired?"

"She wasn't fired from the Citizenship School. She was a school teacher in Charleston when they fired her, and before that, she taught elementary school right here on Johns Island. But that was long before the Citizenship Schools. She started the Citizenship Schools to teach us how to stand up for our rights so we could vote. But when they started the schools, they found out so many of us couldn't even read. So those who couldn't read learned how and we all learned how to stand up for our rights."

"We studied the Voting Rights act this year in Ms. Ervin's class."

"There wouldn't have been no voting rights act if they hadn't started the citizenship schools. Before then, Black people could get lynched trying to vote. In 1954, we started meeting secretly to teach ourselves how to read and how to pass those ridiculous literacy tests they made us take. Just to vote! It took the White folks a long time to figure out how so many of us were learning to read and how we were able to pass the tests since they knew many of us didn't have much formal education."

"Did you, grandma?"

"I knew how to read, but no, I did not have much formal education when I was a child."

"Why?"

"Because we had to work the farm. And for a long time, the only public schools for Black children only went to the eighth grade. Mrs. Clark's parents scraped together the money so she could go to the private high school for Black children, and she also worked to helped pay for it."

"For high school?"

"Yes, baby. There were no public high schools for us

back then," she said and paused. "So, it puzzles me how so many of us running around ashamed of where we come from. How you gonna be ashamed when for so many generations your people struggled and fought to get an education? During slavery, we even went midnight schools!"

"What's a midnight school?"

"It's the school my great-grandmother, Viola, your great-great-great-grandmother, went to to learn to read. You know she was seventeen when emancipation came, and after working hard all day – sixteen hour days sometimes – Viola and the rest stole away at night when it was dark and that ole master thought they were sleeping, and they taught themselves to read!"

What? My great-great-great-grandmother was a slave!

Mama Roxie kept talking, but I couldn't hear her. Like a tidal wave bearing down on whatever was in its path, despair and shame washed over me and took me out.

"And Viola taught her children to read and Cora Mae, my grandmother, taught her children and when we weren't working the fields, my mama taught me."

"My—" I started the sentence, but I couldn't finish it.

"Go on baby."

"—My great-great-great-grandmother was— she was enslaved?"

"Yes."

"Is there— do you have any pictures of her?"

"There aren't any pictures of her, but there are pictures of her daughter and her husband." Mama Roxie looked at me. "What is it, baby?"

"I didn't know we had— I didn't know my—"

"You think what *she* did was something. One little boy, Thomas Johnson bought a blue back speller, the old spelling book, and he tricked his master's son into teaching him to read." She clasped her hands together and smiled as though she'd just learned one of her grandchildren was going to be named class president.

"You know they would give a slave child to their own children to use as a playmate. So, at night when the master's son was studying his lesson, little Thomas would pick out a word he didn't know how to spell and he'd tell him, 'bet you can't spell this!' After the boy spelled the word, Thomas would leave the room and spell the word over and over until he knew how to spell it. He'd also encourage the boy to read his lesson out loud and when he did, little Thomas would compliment him and make him feel so good. Then he'd ask him to read it again. All the while, young Thomas was learning how to read.

"The women who tended to the children also did whatever it took to learn. One woman was so slick, she'd call her mistress's child over and tell her she'd keep her place for her. She held that child in her arms and kept her place for her, and while the child read, she learned to read! Then she taught all her children. So don't tell me—" Mama Roxie shook her head left and right "—Black children can't read! And Jasmine, don't tell me we have anything to be ashamed of."

I could hear my heart beating, it was so quiet. I could also hear myself breathing. My breaths were hard. Angry. Inside, I was summer, fall, winter and spring all rolled up into one season. I did feel ashamed, I guess, but I was also proud. Proud my great-great-great-grandmother taught herself to read. Even though. . .

I looked over at Mama Roxie. *How can you just sit there and keep weeding? After telling me this!* A hot, violent summer storm was brewing inside me, and I didn't know how to stop it. I wanted to hit something. Somebody!

"What'd you say?" She spoke without even looking up. I stared at her in horror! She raised her head and smiled her chipmunk smile. I need to calm down, I thought. I'll use Ms. Evin's breathing trick. I closed my eyes and slowed my breathing, but that didn't help at all. Now I felt like a mucked up winter day. A cold, gray, depressing I-wish-I-were-dead winter day.

She pulled off her gloves, wiped her brow and waited for me to speak. I looked into her eyes, and I knew that whatever I was feeling, whatever I needed to say would be okay with her. My words were barely audible as they forced their way through the tiny opening in my throat.

"Wasn't it against the law?"

"Against the law?"

"For us to learn?"

"If they found out, you were punished. Some were even killed."

My shame and despair about my great-great-great-grandmother quickly morphed into anger when I thought about what she had to go through. Just to learn to read! Mama Roxie shifted her body and smoothed out her dress.

"Years later, here and throughout the south, we had to do the same thing with the Citizenship Schools 'cause they were still trying to keep us from being educated. Now everybody running around here trying to figure out how to save little black children. Teach them how to read!" Mama Roxie waved an angry hand across her face. Then she looked me in the eye. "Baby, we know how to educate our children."

By the time we got home that night, I was exhausted. In addition to going shopping for the party on Saturday, we stopped by the Avery Research Center for African American History and Culture, where Septima Clark had gone to school. Back then, it was called Avery Normal Institute and it was a private college-prep high school for African Americans.

It was named a historical landmark and turned into a research center about twenty years ago. And I couldn't

believe it— I actually saw a picture of Septima Clark and
Rosa Parks sitting together when Rosa Parks was young. The
only pictures I'd ever seen of Rosa Parks were when she had
salt and pepper hair and glasses! In this picture, she wasn't
wearing glasses and her hair was jet black. And she looked so
young.

I washed my face, brushed my teeth, and after kissing
Grandma good night, I collapsed onto my bed. I had wanted
to text Ebonee earlier, but I didn't. Hearing those words
was bad enough, but to actually write, *My great-great-
great-grandmother was a slave!*

CHAPTER 12

I was helping Mama Roxie can beans when my mom called. Mama Roxie told her how much she was enjoying having me here, what a great gardener I was and how much she was going to miss me when I left. "Yes!" she said and paused. "Um hmm, we're canning beans right now. You're gonna have to send her down here every summer." For several seconds, Mama Roxie didn't speak, she just listened. "Hold on a minute," she said and put the phone against her chest. "Jasmine, go around to the side of the house and bring me the blue bucket."

"Yes mam." Mama Roxie put the phone back up to her ear the minute the screen door closed shut.

"There's a lot of hurt in that child. I know you and Calvin love Jasmine and Dalani, but unless you sit down as a family, things aren't going to get any better. I know you have a piece of paper that says you're divorced, but the heart of a child knows otherwise. There are some things you and Calvin need to make right so she can begin to heal. And you need to do it sooner than at once and quicker than right now."

The second she stopped talking, I ran to get the bucket. She was still on the phone when I got back. I put the bucket next to the sink, and Mama Roxie said goodbye to my mom and handed me the phone. I'd only spoken with her once since I'd been here. It was just after we'd landed. She was happy that I'd had a safe flight, and she said she knew I'd be fine on my own.

I'd told her how hot it was when I got off the plane and I thanked her again for the iPod. Now I filled her in on how peaceful it was down here and how much I loved gardening. When I told her what happened with Peter, she told me about the time Mama Roxie begged her not to kill a bug. She We were living in Mears projects then and I was a baby, and mom said Mama Roxie told her to let it crawl onto a piece of paper so she could put it outside.

"Did you kill it?"

"No. But I wanted to," my mom said in a whisper as though she thought Mama Roxie could hear her. Then she told me that she'd made an appointment to meet with two women who were running a rite of passage program called *Sisters in Spirit.* Of course, I had a million questions. She had just as many answers.

"On Sundays for about five hours."

"We meet for five hours!" She couldn't see the scowl on my face, and she didn't bothering responding to my protests.

"You learn history, you'll study African dance. Other kinds of dance too, they said."

"*Every* Sunday?"

Generally three Sundays out of the month. You have discussions with the other girls and with the program directors about what's going on in your lives with school, boys." She paused. "Being young African American and Latino girls and all that comes with that."

"Who are the other girls?"

"I don't know. We'll find out when we meet."

"We?"

"Yes, we. I mean, Sunday is your time unless they need us to help out with something, but parents also meet and talk about how we can support you. We don't just turn you over— we're involved. However they need us to be."

"Oh."

"And how we can support each other too, as parents."

I listened to everything she said. It actually sounded like it'd be cool.

"This is gonna be good for you, Jasmine. Ms. Ervin told me about them last week, and I spoke with Iya Makeba on Wednesday.

"Iya Makeba?"

"Iya means great mother in Yoruba, a West African language. It's a title, like Ms. or Dr. Oh, you'll also have work to do," my mom remembered suddenly. "At your closing ceremony in two years, you'll have a guest speaker, and she said you girls are responsible for getting the speaker. So you'll be working with the other girls learning how to get along and work together."

"We're in it for two years?"

"Yes mam. Or longer depending on you girls and when

you're ready to become young women."

"Where is it?"

"Way out in Brooklyn."

"How will I get out there?"

"Don't worry about that. We'll get you there."

"Now who is we?"

"We is me. Sometimes we might be one of the other parents." She said the meeting was next Thursday after she got off work. I told her about our trip to the Avery Research Center and asked if she'd heard of Septima Clark. She said she'd heard of Septima Clark, but didn't really know much about her. There was a lot she didn't know about our history, she said, but she was going to learn. We were going to learn together.

I hesitated before I asked her if she knew that dad's great-great-grandmother had been enslaved. Before I could ask her if there were any surprises like that on her side of the family, she said she hadn't done her family genealogy. And "yes," she said "I knew your dad's great-great grandmother was a slave. How do you feel, knowing that?"

"I wish I could see a picture of her," I said. "If I had known last week—" my throat tightened up and refused to let me speak. A high-pitched wail escaped anyway, and I mumbled through my tears. "—I would have said a prayer for her."

"Ohhhh sweetie. We can say a prayer for her now."

"Can we do it when you come?" I whispered. "I don't want to do it over the phone."

"Yes."

"And maybe dad—" I decided not to go there. Instead, I told my mom what Mama Roxie had said about Black people needing a healing. She said she'd been in an intense workshop for the past two days where they'd talked about the same thing – Black people needing to heal from the trauma of slavery. From the ancestral memory of the trauma.

"That workshop was a real eye-opener for me." She paused. "It really was."

"How?" I asked. "How do we get over slavery?"

"By learning the truth and talking about it. Like what Ms. Ervin did with you all last week. And remembering the good in us. Celebrating the good." I wiped my eyes again and tried to steady my breathing. Then I closed my eyes and waited for my mom to say something that would take away the hurt.

"In the workshop, they told us how we'd taken in a lot of nasty, evil stuff that didn't belong to us. They said we need to get it out so we can stop acting crazy with all this skin color prejudice. Fighting each other!"

"What about White people?"

"They're a different kind of crazy," she said. "They have a lot of work to do. A lot of work."

I wished my mom a safe flight and told her I'd see her and Dalani tomorrow. Then I handed the phone to Mama

Roxie. As soon as she hung up, she scooped me up in her arms and held me like a newborn baby. My chest heaved and my upper body bobbed up and down against her chest.

"It's all right, baby. It's all right," Grandma said as she rocked me gently from side to side. Then, in a soft, sweet whisper almost, she began to sing. "Ain't you got a right. Ain't you got a right. Ain't you got a right to the tree of life.

"Ain't you got a right. Ain't you got a right. Ain't you got a right to the tree of life. Jasmine has a right. Jasmine has a right. Jasmine has a right to the tree of life. Yes, Jasmine has a right, Jasmine has a right. Jasmine has a right to the tree of life." For a few seconds more, she cradled me. Then, ever so gently, she kissed me on my forehead and told me to go wash my face.

I rubbed my eyes dry as I walked to the bathroom. As soon as I closed the door I came face to face with my reflection. My eyes were puffy and tired. I stared in the mirror and wondered if I resembled my great-great-great-grandmother. She had to be dark like me since all my aunts and uncles were dark. Mama Roxie was dark. I thought about how light my mom and Aunt Angie were and how light her father was. And my great-grandma Sally, who died when I was nine. She had white skin and green eyes. White skin? My brain cells were starting to hurt. I didn't want to think about it anymore.

I took a deep breath in. I turned the handle for hot water, then the one for cold. The warm water felt good on my face, and I didn't care if I also wet my hair. I hadn't really thought much about my hair since I'd been down here.

I walked back into the kitchen and heard a car pulling into the driveway. The rocks crackled underneath the tires until the car came to a halt. The engine ceased its murmuring and the car door slammed shut. Mama Roxie looked out the kitchen window and a huge Grinch smile broke out all over her face. I listened to the forceful, intentional sound of heels striking the concrete walkway. Whoever was coming walked as though they were somebody important. Somebody on a mission.

"Knock! Knock! Knock! Mama Simmons?"

Mama Roxie flung open the screen door. "Oh Lord. You surprised me. I didn't think I'd see you until tomorrow." A beautiful, towering, dark-skinned woman wearing an olive green and black dress, with gold trim and matching headdress made her entrance into the kitchen. Her locs cascaded down her shoulders and reached down to her lower back.

She leaned over and kissed Mama Roxie on the cheek. Then she disappeared her in her arms. As she released Mama Roxie from her bosom, Mama Roxie kissed the woman hard on her cheek.

"And who is this beautiful young girl with the gorgeous

smile?"

"I told her her smile was so bright, it could warm the sun," Mama Roxie said in that way that made you proud you were her granddaughter. "This is Jasmine, my grandbaby from Harlem, USA, like they like to say. Jasmine, this is Sister Muhsinah."

"Hi Jasmine, I've heard so much about you— and Dalani. Is he here too?"

"He'll be here tomorrow," I said as Sister Muhsinah walked over to me. She leaned over and planted on a kiss on my face. And even though I didn't know her, I didn't mind.

"Sit down!" Mama Roxie waved her hand in the direction of the kitchen table and all three of us pulled up a chair. "What brings you here? You dressed like you got to be somewhere."

"I was on my way to Avery."

"We were there yesterday, but we only stayed a few minutes. I told Jasmine maybe she and Dalani could go back Saturday."

"You didn't see any of the exhibits?" Sister Muhsinah directed her question to me.

"No, mam." I wanted to tell her about the picture I'd seen of Rosa Parks and Septima Clark, but I couldn't take my thoughts off how beautiful she was. How beautiful her skin was. It was so dark, but it was beautiful! She was beautiful. Like a high fashion model. I'd never seen anyone who was that dark *and* that beautiful.

"Earl had to pick up something, so we peeked in and saw the replica of the school room."

"I'm meeting some of my students, and we're going to view the Priscilla exhibit. I'd love to have Jasmine join us."

"The little slave girl?" Mama Roxie asked?

"Uh huh." Muhsinah turned to me. "A ten-year-old little girl kidnapped from Sierra Leone. They were able to actually find some of her descendants, and they went to Sierra Leone three years ago. So there's a photo exhibit about their trip and about Priscilla."

Mama Roxie looked over at me. "Would you like to go?"

"Yes," I said excited about the prospects of spending time with Muhsinah and meeting kids my age."

"Are you leaving now, or can you stay a minute?"

"Actually, I'm running a little late. I just left Alberta, and I have some of her baskets. Can I leave them with you until she gets settled. I told her you wouldn't mind."

"Of course! Do you need some help carrying them?"

"That would be great."

"Jasmine, help Sister Muhsinah," Mama Roxie said as they both got up from the table. "She still not settled?"

Sister Muhsinah closed her eyes and shook her head no.

"That's a shame."

As soon as we'd put the baskets in Grandma's den, I ran to the bathroom to fix my hair. I gathered it into a bun and put a pink scrunchy around it. Then I smoothed it over with oil to try to make it look better. Mama Roxie had promised to wash and press it for me tonight, so I'd be cute for the party.

Sister Muhsinah was a science teacher, but every summer, she ran an African American History camp at Avery. On the drive into Charleston, she told me that Alberta's baskets were made out of sweetgrass that grew throughout the area and down into Florida. Alberta had learned how to make baskets when she was a child, and now she sold her baskets all over the world. She said we brought basket making over here with us from Africa.

Then she told me Alberta and her family had been kicked off their land six years ago and had moved to the northern part of Johns Island to start over. They were living in a trailer now and she needed a lot more space for her baskets.

The same thing had happened to another family who lived in the southern part of Johns Island and also to a family in a place along the Cainhoy peninsula, Sister Muhsinah said. All along the coast of South Carolina and Georgia, families had lost their land. Alberta and her husband William had lived in their house for 45 years, and the land the house was built on had been in William's family since 1868.

"That's just three years after slavery," I said, shocked.

"Yup! Slavery. Reconstruction. Forty acres and a mule." Sister Muhsinah shook her head and forced out a sigh.

"Nothing lasts forever."

For a long while, she didn't speak. I could tell she didn't really want to talk about why Alberta and William had been forced off their land, but I wanted to know. We drove under the same canopy of trees Uncle Earl and I had driven under when he picked me up from the airport. Both times, I noticed several orange strings tied around some of the trees along the highway. I decided to break the somber silence riding shotgun with us.

"What are those orange strings tied around the trees?"

"It means the land has been sold, but those trees are protected, so they can't cut them down."

I figured out a way to steer the conversation back to Alberta and William. "Did those people who lost their land live in all-Black towns?"

Sister Muhsinah shook her head no. "All the land in this area was formerly lived on and cared for by people we now call Indians. Indigenous people," she said, again shaking her head. "You have to forgive me, Jasmine. It's just hard— seeing what keeps happening."

Sister Muhsinah didn't seem tired when I first met her, but thinking about Alberta and William seemed to be draining all her energy. We'd studied forty acres and a mule in social studies, but I played dumb and asked her about it anyway.

"Ms. Alberta lost forty acres of her land?"

"No," she said and proceeded to give me a history lesson dating back to the Civil War. "So, before the Civil War ended, General Sherman met with Black men and asked them literally, what are we going to do with all of you, now that you've fought in the war and earned your freedom. They said, we need some land." She looked over at me. "Makes sense right?"

"Yeah."

"We don't need to be taken care of. Give us land and we'll take care of ourselves. We've been working it forever. Right?" She asked as she nodded her head yes. "We took care of you all, right? For a couple hundred years! Now let us take care of ourselves. So he issued an order saying that formerly enslaved families would be given forty acres of land to work and live on. The army had a surplus of mules they no longer needed so Sherman threw them in too. A year later, about ten thousand Blacks had settled on about four-hundred thousand acres of land in Georgia and South Carolina."

"That's when Ms. Alberta's ancestors got their land?"

"Nope! President Johnson – Lincoln had been assassinated – said uh uh, we can't have this, and he forced all the Black people off the land and gave it back to the White folk who'd stolen it from the indigenous." Sister Muhsinah paused long enough to frown. "William's great-great-grandfather worked as a sharecropper and somehow was able to save up enough money until he could buy land. Most of the land we bought back then was marsh land White folks didn't want because they didn't think you could grow anything on it, and there were way too many mosquitoes for them. Today, all up and down this coast, those marsh lands are fancy resorts like Hilton Head Island— making White folk rich."

"So they're going to build a resort where Alberta's land used to be?"

"William's great-great-grandfather bought farm land further inland. That land had been in the family almost one-hundred and fifty years. William even has a copy of the original deed from 1868."

"Then, how did they lose it?"

"So the land is owned by many descendants. We call it heirs' property. There might be three generations of people who own, say eighteen acres of land, land that has been passed down, a lot of times, without a will. But if one person wants to sell his portion of the eighteen acres, the way the law is set up, it forces the other people to have to sell too. It's the biggest scam going, and it's tearing families apart. And making the rich richer." Sister Muhsinah adjusted the air conditioner. Then she continued. "What they do is they find the one heir, usually someone living in New York or somewhere else far away, who really doesn't have ties to the land, and they get them to sell."

"Why can't that one family member just sell their part of the land to everybody else?"

"Jasmine, honey, this land is land that wealthy developers want and its worth a hundred times more than what our ancestors paid for it years ago. Family members can't afford to buy the land at what it sells for today. I just read that African Americans have lost fourteen million of the fifteen million acres of land we owned since Emancipation. Fourteen million!" She shook her head.

Wait, Ms. Ervin just taught us this. But hearing about it happening to someone my grandmother and Sister Muhsinah knew. . . "But, if the land is worth so much money, why wouldn't everyone want to sell it?" I asked. "I mean, if it's worth so much."

"The developers aren't offering to pay what it's actually worth. It's worth even a hundred times more than what they're offering. But to answer your question, families are living on land that's been in their family for generations— like I said, dating back to slavery or just after slavery. These developers see land as a source of wealth, but Jasmine, we see it as a source of life."

Sister Muhsinah's phone beeped. "It's probably Reggie making sure I'm on my way," she said as she opened the text message. She phoned Reggie and told him we were about ten minutes away. Then she came back to our discussion. "So, in Africa land never belonged to one person, it belonged to the family— the extended family. That's how we lived, and we brought that with us when we came here."

Sister Muhsinah slowed down for a stop light. "On Johns Island, people work three and four jobs to pay their taxes to keep their land. We're not rich people, financially, but land *is* wealth. It's wealth because it gives you a place to call home. The same place your parents and their parents called home. Knowing you have a place to live that's yours, that no one can take from you—" Sister Muhsinah looked over at me, "—there were six of us, and when we were growing up, we'd go without Christmas presents because it was more important for daddy to pay his taxes so we could have a place to live than it was to get presents."

I understood why this was so painful for Sister Muhsinah. I was going to tell her I got what she was saying and ask her if anything could be done to keep people from losing their land, but my phone rang. What? It was my father. He'd gotten in the night before, but he said it was too late to call. He wanted to spend some time with me before the party tomorrow, and Mama Roxie told him I was on my way to Avery. He asked if he could meet me there.

CHAPTER 13

A ten-year-old girl living in Sierra Leone, minding her business, was kidnapped and taken to a castle on Bunce Island off the coast of Sierra Leone. The castle was owned and managed by different British corporations, the placard read. It said they held her there until they put her on a ship called the Hare. What a stupid name for a ship, I thought. On April ninth, 1756, she and eighty-three other "slaves" began their voyage.

"They weren't slaves," I said out loud as I read the placard. "She was a ten-year old girl!" Sister Muhsinah walked over and put her arm around me. She stood with me as I read the rest of the placard: "Sixteen of the eighty-four Africans died during the ten-week journey to Charleston."

When we got to the Avery Research Center, I met six of Sister Muhsinah's students. Three were my age, one girl, Fatimata, was ten and had just finished the fifth grade, and there were two twin boys aged eleven. This was their first meeting of the summer and they all seemed excited about the two-week long African American History Camp.

I found out that Fatimata was Sister Muhsinah's niece. She looked a lot like her. She had beautiful dark skin, just like Sister Muhsinah, and she wore her hair in twists. Her twists really looked good on her. I wondered if kids teased her because she wore her hair natural and whether it bothered her if they did? Or whether they teased her because she was dark-skinned? They probably didn't, I thought, since her skin was so beautiful.

The first thing we saw as we entered the exhibit hall was a huge poster with the words, *Finding Priscilla's Children* written at the top. Below the words was a drawing of a little brown-skinned girl sandwiched in between two much taller men. All three of them were chained together with ropes tied around their necks and around both wrists. You couldn't see the men's faces, just their chests since they were so tall and the girl was so little. Her hair was in braids that just reached her shoulders. She looked terrified. All three were walking in tall weeds and the sky was a perfect summer-day blue.

As I read about the ten-year-old girl whose real name, nobody knew, I wondered what her mother and father did when they found out she was gone. Maybe they were kidnapped too, I thought. *So, it wasn't just over here that mothers had their children ripped out of their arms and sold away. All so some greedy, evil people could make money.* I couldn't stop shaking my head.

Some asshole named Elias Ball II, bought her, I read. *That doesn't even sound right, 'bought her.'* He had purchased three boys and two girls for 600 pounds. "A wealthy South Carolina rice plantation owner," they called him. Why couldn't they write the truth? Why didn't it say, Elias Ball II, who was engaged in human trafficking, buying children kidnapped from their parents and grandparents, then enslaving them! And her name wasn't Priscilla, I screamed inside! The little girl who'd been kidnapped, sold into slavery and renamed Priscilla married a man named Jeffrey, and they had ten children. They think only four lived to be adults. *I wonder what happened to the other six?* The last placard I read said she had thirty grandchildren and she died in 1811.

Still no sign of my dad. Why would he call and say he was going to meet me and not show up? And why was I surprised? "Have you looked at the photos?" Sister Muhsinah asked. I forgot she was standing beside me. We walked to the photo gallery mounted on the wall and took in the large-sized color photographs of Africans, African Americans and White People who had traveled to Sierra Leone three years ago.

Thomalind Polite, Priscilla's great-great-great-great-great-granddaughter, discovered she was a descendant of Priscilla when one of Elias Ball's descendants did a genealogical search and wrote a book about his ancestors. She and her husband and her daughter were invited to Sierra Leone by the country's leaders. The people in Sierra Leone said that Ms. Polite coming to Sierra Leone was like Priscilla coming back home.

After we looked at the photos, Sister Muhsinah announced we'd be leaving soon, and afterward, we were going out to eat to discuss the exhibit. She told us that we'd pass by Denmark Vesey's home on our way to the restaurant and we could take pictures if we wanted.

Just before it was time to go, I read about the Triangular Slave Trade. Traders from Newport, Rhode Island, Salem, Massachusetts, New London, Connecticut and New York frequently traveled to Bunce Island to purchase Africans and take them to the West Indies or directly to South Carolina. *New York! I didn't know New York was involved.*

They called it the triangular trade because Northern slave traders often purchased African men, women and children with rum manufactured in New England with sugar and molasses the manufacturers had purchased from the West Indies. It was so wack since Africans had been sold to planters in the West Indies to the harvest the sugar and the molasses that would then be used to make the very same rum the slave traders used to purchase them! Purchased with rum! I shook my head and sucked my teeth at the thought. *Who would trade people for some rum?*

We left the air-conditioned exhibit hall and stepped outside into the sweltering summer sun. My phone beeped. *Maybe this is my dad.*

It was a text from Ebonee. She said she wished Chilaun lived in New York. She said he wasn't trying to get in her pants, like the boys in New York, and he respected her for who she was and not just because she was fine. I texted her back.

"Date Sekou. He's not like that."

"He's 2 serious."

"Not all the time."

Now my phone was ringing.

"Mom?" She began by telling me not to get upset, that everything was okay. "The hospital? What happened?" My dad was on his way to meet me when a car hit him. "He got hit by a car," I screamed. No, my mom told me. He *almost* got hit by a car while he was riding Uncle Elijah's motorcycle. At first, he was unconscious, but he's okay now. He has a broken leg, and he suffered a concussion. They want to keep him overnight, but he's okay. My mom told me that Uncle Earl was on his way to Avery to pick me up.

***

When I walked into my dad's hospital room, his eyes were closed. His right leg was in a cast and the right side of his face was bruised and swollen. Uncle Earl and I sat on opposite sides of his bed, and I watched him as he lay there sleeping. All those plans I had for ignoring him at Mama Roxie's party were gone now. I took out my Sidekick to text Ebonee. I'd promised her I would when I got to the hospital.

"Jazzy." My dad had opened his eyes and was smiling at me.

"Daddy are you okay?"

"Hey Calvin."

My dad looked over at Uncle Earl. "Earl," he said and smiled again. Then, he looked back at me. "I'm all right. How was the exhibit?"

"It was good," I said not really wanting to talk about the exhibit. "You got hit by a car?"

"Almost. Almost. I saw it coming and dropped my bike. So, how are you? I heard you have a green thumb and Mama's loved having you."

"Yes."

My dad turned and locked eyes with Uncle Earl. "Man, they trying to keep me here overnight. You know I ain't trying to miss the party."

"We'll be by to get you tomorrow morning. I'ma go downstairs to the cafeteria. You want anything?"

"I'm good."

"Jasmine, can I get you something?"

"No thank you."

Uncle Earl left me and my dad alone. I hadn't been alone with him in— it had been almost a year I thought as I counted up the months. My dad asked me to pull my chair closer. Then, he reached out his hand and waited. I bowed my head, not wanting to stare at his bruised face. My breathing became deeper. My stomach started expanding, then contracting, and I could feel the evil part of me moving around inside. *Even your father didn't want Your Black Ass.*

"Jazzy?" He moved his hand a half-inch closer. I just

sat there, staring at my own hands. Breathing hard. "I haven't done right by you. Or Dalani."

"I know." My eyes were wet now. He took a deep breath in and blew it out slowly.

"Your mom told me about *Sisters in Spirit*. They sound like a great group." I nodded my agreement then blinked back the first of several tiny tears struggling to break free. He waited for me to say something, and I waited for him. "So, there's a meeting next Thursday. I'll get there a few minutes late, but I'll be there." My head snapped in his direction. "I want to be there," he said. "I wanted—"

"—Then why weren't you?" He stared at me, but he didn't say anything. I studied his face, his dark chocolate skin. I'd never noticed it before, but his eyes and my eyes were a lot alike. And he had the longest eyelashes for a man.

"Jasmine, I've been dealing with some stuff. But things are different now."

"I mean, I know today, you were in an accident, but all those others times. Why should I believe you?"

"You shouldn't. Not until you see me walking through the door. And when you see me, then you can start trusting me again." His ebony eyes said he was telling the truth, but they'd been known to lie before.

A numb silence filled the room.

He reached out his hand again, and this time, however reluctantly, I reached back. His hand was warm. And strong.

And big, just like I remembered. It was the same hand that walked me to school when I was in kindergarten and first grade. The same hand that used to grab me and tickle me as I squealed at the top of my lungs whenever we went to the big park down the street from where we lived. I called it the big park since it was ten times bigger than the park at Mears projects.

My dad used to play this game with me and Dalani where we'd run and he'd catch us, grab us under his arms, carry us back to where mom was sitting then tickle us until we escaped and started running again. She'd be saying, 'Jasmine, Dalani, run, run,' and he'd be tickling us, and we'd all be laughing.

I could feel my dad searching me with his eyes. And I sensed him wanting me to respond. "I didn't know we were descendants of people who had been enslaved," I said finally.

"Yes. Your great-great-great-grandmother was a slave."

"Enslaved." I waited to be chastised for correcting him. His silence only made me bolder. "They weren't slaves. They were Africans. Before they came here—" I paused, "before they were brought here. They were iron workers and rice farmers." My voice trailed off. "And ten-year-old little girls."

He nodded as if he'd just learned something that made a lot of sense. "You're right," he said, still nodding.

"So, we'll remember great-great-grandma Viola on Saturday."

"Mom told you?"

He shook his head yes. "Could you get my wallet?" He pointed to the nightstand. "Next to the phone." I handed him his wallet, and he pulled out a picture and handed it to me.

"When was this?"

"You were three. That was your favorite toy. It was taken right after your third birthday." My dad smiled. Then winced. "It might be time to take the pain medication," he said and winced again. I handed the picture back to him. "I keep this one because that's the year," he hesitated, "I was out of work. Six months. It was just you and me all day. You remember that?"

"A little."

"I'd take you to the park and all you wanted was to go up and down the slide."

That seemed like such a long time ago, I thought and looked over at my dad. "I remember when you used to tickle us. In the park." He smiled. Then, he blinked back his first tiny tear.

"So, I got you something. I was going to take you to my favorite restaurant downtown and give it to you there." My dad handed me a bag, and I pulled out a black T-shirt. "It's your mom's favorite restaurant, too. Maybe Saturday."

"I AM ENOUGH," I said reading the front of the shirt out loud. The words were written in three-inch block letters. Pink letters. They stood out perfectly against the black form-fitted cotton T-shirt. On the back were the words, "I AM," in white letters, then underneath, in increasingly darker shades of pink and increasingly larger letters, "Safe, Special, Healthy, Peaceful, Loveable, Beautiful, Powerful," and lastly, "ENOUGH!"

"It says I'm beautiful enough."

"It says you're safe enough, special enough, healthy enough. I hope you're healthy. You been eating your vegetables?

"Yes."

"Peaceful, loveable, powerful and yes, beautiful!"

I looked up at my dad and I looked past his loving smile.

"Mom says you married her because she's light-skinned."

"Jasmine," my father began as he reached over and grabbed my hand. "I married your mother because I loved her. And because I wanted to spend the rest of my life with her."

"What about me?"

I watched his eyes fill with a clear glaze. "Jasmine, I've been going through a lot of stuff that has absolutely nothing to do with you or Dalani. You hear me?" I just sat there as he squeezed my hand. His voiced cracked when he squeezed tighter. "Huh?"

"Yes," I whispered.

"I'm not going anywhere," he began as he shook his

head side-to-side. "You have me—" for a second, my father's words got stuck in his throat and made him mute "—for the rest of your life! I'm the one Black man you can count on. I know I haven't been. But you just know that from now on, I am."

After he let go of my hand, I got up and went into the bathroom to put on my T-shirt. My scrunchy matches my shirt, I thought as I checked myself out in the mirror. I AM ENOUGH! I stared at those words and broke out into a smile as a voice began dancing around in my head. Not the evil voice that had been haunting me forever, but my dad's voice singing *"Ebony Eyes!"*

"Does it fit?"

"Yes," I yelled as I slid my scrunchy off, smoothed back my hair, held tightly to a fistful, then put the scrunchy back on. I opened the bathroom door and searched my father's eyes. He smiled and nodded approvingly. I kept waiting for him to stop smiling and say something, but he didn't.

"How do I look?" I asked.

Tears flooded my eyes as my father began to sing *"Ebony Eyes."* For real.

CHAPTER 14

On the drive home, I asked Uncle Earl if we could stop by the store. I wanted to buy my dad a get-well card. That night, Mama Roxie and I baked him a pound cake. After she made the icing, she let me squirt it out to make the flowers and decorate the cake. My dad had a sweet tooth and wouldn't turn down any dessert, but homemade pound cake with vanilla ice cream was his favorite. Mom used to say he was going to clog up his arteries and have a heart attack with all that vanilla ice cream.

It was getting late, late for us anyway, and both Mama Roxie and I wanted to be well rested for her party. She said she was expecting about one-hundred people.

"A hundred!"

"That's what your Aunt Angeline says." She flashed her chipmunk smile. "We have a lot of kin and your aunts and uncles have lots of people they grew up with who are just like family. Some are flying in from California." I'd never seen anyone grin that hard.

"Seriously?"

"And my friends will be here too!"

"Where are you going to put all your presents?"

"I'll find a spot," she said and looked over at me. "But everybody coming is all the present I need. Your father being alive." Mama Roxie shook her head slowly. "I don't care if he eats this whole cake all by himself."

"Grandma, are you crying?"

"They're happy tears, Jasmine." Mama Roxie rubbed her eyes as she breathed out a sigh of relief. I kissed her goodnight and went to bed.

The next morning, Uncle Earl picked up my mom and Dalani from the airport, then stopped by the hospital to get my dad. I was getting dressed for the party when they drove up.

"Jasmine, they're here!"

"Okay!" I took one last look at my hair and smiled. Mama Roxie had gotten up early to fry chicken even though everyone had told her not to. They wanted this to be her special day where she didn't do anything except enjoy herself. I guess they didn't realize that whenever she cooked, she was enjoying herself. After we ate breakfast, she did my hair.

"So, how do you want me to fix it?"

"You're gonna wash it and press it, right?

"Is that what you want?"

"Yes."

"You never wear it natural?"

"No. No mam." I thought about Fatimata's hair and how pretty it looked. Maybe I'd look good in twists. Nope, I could see their faces now. And I could hear them as soon as I walked away: "She needs to do something with that hair."

"I saw a girl at church the other week, and her hair was

so gorgeous and it fit her face so well. Her face was round, just like yours, and I bet I could fix that same style."

"Hers was natural?"

"It was about the same length as yours. She had it braided, about to here—" she placed her hand about three inches back from my ford "—and she had a head band and the rest was natural. And it was so clean and pretty. I can blow it out then braid it. It would really highlight your face."

"You were a beautician?"

"I never got paid to do hair, but I had seven girls!"

"Can you just press it, then I'll style it."

"How about we do this. Let me blow dry it and style it and see how you like it. If you don't like it, then I'll press it."

In about forty-five minutes, she was done. My hair was longer than I thought it would be in the top, and it was really soft. Mama Roxie had braided the front and side parts and the rest was picked out into an afro. Sister Muhsinah had given her a couple of head bands for me and I'd chosen the yellow one to go with my yellow and black outfit. She'd also used rosemary oil she got from Sister Muhsinah, and it smelled great.

I heard Mama Roxie open the kitchen door and head outside. I joined her in time to see Dalani and my mom hopping out of the back of the car. Uncle Earl jumped out of the front and walked to the passenger's side to help my father get out. As soon as dad steadied himself on his crutches, Mama Roxie grabbed him and started to cry.

"Thank you, Jesus. Thank you, thank you, thank you."

"Mama, I'm all right."

"Thank you, Jesus! Thank you."

"Jasmine, look at you!" My mom couldn't stop grinning.

"You look so cute!"

"Yeah. Your hair looks good."

I couldn't believe it. Dalani complimented my hair.

"Well," mom began as she touched the Afro part of my hair. "Do you like it?"

"Yes."

"How long did it take?"

"Not long."

"It's so soft. It looks great on you, Jasmine."

"Thanks."

"You think you'll keep it like this?"

"No," I said quickly.

"You just said you liked it?"

"I can't wear my hair to school like this!"

"Maybe you'll change your mind."

"No," I said while shaking my head to make sure she understood.

"Well, you look beautiful."

I beamed proudly. I do look cute like this, I thought and kept on smiling.

"Come on inside and put your things away." Mama Roxie told me to show my mom and Dalani to their rooms. My mom and I were going to share the bed I'd been sleeping in and Dalani was going to sleep in the adjoining room.

By the time, they'd settled in and had gotten something to eat, it was time to start setting up the tables and chairs for Mama Roxie's one-hundred guests.

Just like she predicted, mad people showed up to wish her a happy eightieth birthday. By three o'clock, our yard was filled with sons and daughters and in-laws and aunts and uncles, great aunts and uncles, and all shapes and sizes of grandchildren, nieces and nephews, and a host of brother Eddies and sister Mae Sues, who weren't blood brothers and sisters but were treated just like family.

I met about twenty-five of my cousins, most of whom lived in South Carolina, but also several from D.C. All my dad's brothers and sisters who used to live in New York had left years ago. They'd come back to South Carolina and built homes since, unlike Alberta and William, they'd been able to keep their property. Mom said dad's grandmother made sure each one of her heirs had individual deeds to their share of the seventy-seven acres that was hers to pass on.

Mama Roxie had been living in her house for the past twenty years, ten of them by herself. She wasn't the only one who'd gotten up early to fry chicken, I thought as I looked at all the food on the table. Even the Chinese Take Out people didn't have this much fried chicken, I thought and shook my head. There was an equal amount of corn on the cob, potato salad, gumbo, barbequed spare ribs, deviled eggs, mac and cheese and of course, Mama Roxie's rolls.

The watermelon was placed on the dessert table along with sweet potato pies, several homemade cakes and one huge birthday cake made by a baker who was a friend of Aunt Angeline. She'd decorated it with a picture of Mama Roxie in the middle, and her full name, Roxie Ella Simmons, and the words *"Happy 80th"* were printed underneath. It was a red velvet cake with cream cheese and pecan icing, and I couldn't wait for her to cut it.

Almost everyone had stuffed their plates with round one and many were heading back for round two when I decided it was time for dessert. My strategy was to start off with a piece of sweet potato pie, but save room for Grandma's cake. I cut the pie and grabbed a plastic fork and a napkin. When I looked up, my dad was hobbling toward me. "We're going to honor your great-great-great grandmother today."

"Today?"

"Your grandmother wants to do it today. Your mom said you wrote something."

"I didn't tell her I was writing anything."

"That's all right," he said and put his arm around my shoulder. "Do you want to say anything?"

"No!" I looked up at him. "Not in front of everybody."

"You don't want to say a prayer for her?"

"I thought it was just gonna be us."

"This is us." He smiled. "Everybody here is family."

"Who are those White people?"

"Mr. Covington and his wife?" He looked in their direction. "He's the man with the horses. They live down the road." He could sense my attitude. "You haven't seen him riding this week?"

"They're going to be here for the ceremony?"

"It looks like it," he said and smiled

"They're family?"

"They're not part of our family, but they're friends of the family, and they came to be with your grandmother on her eightieth birthday." My father waited for me to respond. "Jasmine, let me tell you something it took me a long time to figure out. Holding on to anger and resentment keeps you stuck in a place you don't want to be. And it keeps you from doing what's yours to do."

"And what about them?" He turned in the direction my finger was pointing.

"Oh my god! Mr. and Mrs. Carawan. I can't believe it. They're Mama's friends from a long time ago. I didn't know they were here."

"They just came." I still didn't understand why me and Dalani and mom and dad couldn't just get together as a family and have a ceremony for great-great-great-grandmother Viola.

"They worked on Johns Island with Septima Clark and a man named Esau Jenkins, and I used to play with their son."

"They worked with the Citizenship Schools?"

I was surprised White people had worked in the Citizenship Schools. My dad was surprised I knew what they were.

"Whatchu know about the Citizenship Schools?"

"Mama Roxie told me."

"Yup. They worked in the literacy program, singing songs, writing songs. They put on folk festivals here on the island. They also sang at Civil Rights meetings. You probably don't know about SNCC?"

"Yes, I do. The Student Non-Violent Coordinating Committee. We learned about them this year."

"Good! Well Mr. Carawan sang at their meetings. They recorded some of the choirs on the island too. Oh man!" My dad couldn't contain his happiness. "He was also Septima Clark's chauffeur, driving her all around this island."

"Jasmine!" My mom was waving me and my dad over to where she and Dalani were standing.

"Mom wants us." Dad turned to try to wave to Mr. Carawan and his wife, but they were busy hugging people and they didn't see him.

"You can meet them as soon as Grandma's done."

"Okay," I said as we headed over to mom and Dalani.

She eyed my sweet potato pie. "You're not having any birthday cake?"

"I'm having pie and cake." She shook her head and smiled. "We're doing it now?"

"I think so," she said as she put her arm around me and pulled me close to her.

Uncle Elijah placed a chair near the staging area where a drum set, a guitar and a saxophone sat ready to go, and he waved Mama Roxie over. He handed her the microphone and whispered in her ear.

"Is it working?" Grandma asked as she lightly tapped the mic.

"It's working," Uncle Elijah told her.

"I feel like a celebrity with this microphone."

"You are," someone shouted.

"I want to thank each and every one of you for coming here today to help me celebrate my eightieth birthday. You don't know what a blessing it is to have all of you here." She looked out at all her guests then took a deep breath in.

"Y'all know that my baby, Calvin, was in an accident yesterday. And you also know how good God is." Grandma waited while everyone amened and clapped and thanked Jesus that my dad's accident hadn't been any worse. "So I wanna thank God for Calvin, and for each of you.

"Because instead of lying up in some hospital, or even worse, he's here with us! A little battered and little bruised, but he's here." Mama Roxie pushed a tear out of her way and continued on.

"I asked Sister Muhsinah, who's like a daughter to me, to lead us in honoring another member of our family. It's time we remember those who've come and gone. Those who worked hard and sacrificed so that we could sit where we sit today. It's time we do this, for the grandbabies. And for ourselves. Sister Muhsinah."

Sister Muhsinah walked over and Mama Roxie handed her the mic.

"Good afternoon."

"Good afternoon!"

"So today, we're going to honor Viola Mae Miles who was born into slavery in 1848 and emancipated at age seventeen." She waited as unsuspecting family members took in the weight of her words. The whisperings and murmurings were quickly followed by "shhhhh, shhhhh" as everyone was eager to hear what would come next.

"Now, many families are ashamed of their ancestry. They don't talk about the past. Well, today, we're silent no more. Today, we remember. Today, we want to honor great-great-great-grandmother Viola— to some of you. Great-great-grandmother to others, and just great-grandmother to our queen mother, Mama Simmons, also known as Mama Roxie." She looked over at Mama Roxie. "Or, just plain mama," she said as Mama Roxie's face lit up.

"So, we'll honor her today, by speaking her name. And as we call out the name of Viola Mae Miles, we want to let her know that we're here. We want to let her know that we're strong. We want to let her know that we re-mem-ber! That we're not ashamed to remember. That we're her proud descendants.

"We know that her seeds were planted long, long ago, and that some seeds fell in the pathway and got stomped on, and they didn't grow. But many seeds fell on fertile ground and they multiplied a thousand fold." Sister Muhsinah paused, pointed. Then, in a whisper, said, "You are those seeds."

I took a deep breath in and cleared my eyes as she continued on in her normal speaking voice. "And as you continue to grow and blossom, be proud of where you come from! Be proud of your ancestors! And know that the pain of the past and hope of the future are rooted in the same soil."

Hands began clapping and voices released whatever they needed to release. Dalani leaned over and asked my dad why he'd never told us about our great-great-great-grandmother. I couldn't hear his answer because Mama Roxie started talking again. She told everyone what she'd told me about great-great-great-grandmother Viola going to the midnight school and how she taught her children to read.

She said our family had so much to be proud of and

nothing to be ashamed of. And when she paused, it began —
with one lone voice, somewhere in the middle of our family
gathering. And, after the first two words, "A-a-ma-zi-ing
grace—" as if we were a church choir that had rehearsed
this past Wednesday night, everybody sang "—how sweet
the sound."

And we continued on until the last note was sung. "That
saved a wretch like me. I once was lost, but now I'm found.
Was blind, but now I see. T'was Grace that taught my heart
to fear. And Grace, my fears relieved. How precious did that
Grace appear the hour I first believed. Through many
dangers, toils and snares we have already come. T'was Grace
that brought us safe thus far and Grace will lead us home.
When we've been here ten thousand years bright shining as
the sun. We've no less days to sing God's praise then when
we've first begun."

"Hallelujah! Hallelujah! Hallelujah!"

"Many of you know that that song was written by a slave
trader, John Newton, on board one of his vessels as he had a
change of heart about his chosen profession." Sister
Muhsinah was speaking again. It sounded like she was
preaching, actually. "What they don't tell you is the music,
the music that gets down in your bones every time you hear
it, is from you. Your people!"

"That's right!"

"Those who know — musicologists they call themselves —

they know that melody to be from West Africa."

"Say so!"

"It's a mournful West African chant. One that some say Mr. Newton heard as your ancestors cried out from the hull of that ship they were on!"

"Yes suh!"

"So, musicologists believe that although he may have written the words, our people wrote the melody!"

"That's right!"

"We moaned and we chanted on board those ships, because even though you can chain the body, you can never chain the spirit!"

"That's right!"

"Hallelujah!"

"Even though you can chain the body, you can never chain Spirit!"

"Preach!"

Sister Muhsinah paused while we all affirmed and amened her words. And when the clapping and the shouting died down, she began again – this time in a quieter voice. "So, it's no accident that you re-mem-ber that song today as we re-mem-ber our ancestors." She paused again. "So now, I invite everyone to call out the names of your people, your ancestors. Remember them. Honor them. Thank them. Forgive them. Love them."

Sister Muhsinah placed the microphone on an empty

chair. My aunts and uncles and older cousins began to speak the names of the Simmonses and the Fullers and the Mileses who had long since passed on. Some began to weep. Others started to pray. I watched them all – with moist eyes and a bittersweet heart.

Then I closed my eyes and whispered my great-great-great-grandmother Viola's name. When I opened them, I watched as mom and dad eyed each other. He moved first, reaching out for Dalani, then for me. Mom did the same. And I placed one hand in his hand and the other in hers. Dalani did the same. And we chained our hands together in a circle, me and Dalani, and mom and dad. And on Mama Roxie's eightieth birthday, under a South Carolina sun, on a July fourth sky-blue summer day, we said a prayer for great-great-great-grandmother, Viola Mae Miles.

Firmly rooted now
I blossom in love's beauty
I'm kissed by the sun

CHAPTER 15

I rolled over and stared at the color photo sitting on top of my desk. It was me, Mama Roxie and Sister Muhsinah at Mama Roxie's eightieth birthday party. *I wish I could go there every summer... My great-great-great-grandmother was freed at 17, and she learned how to read in a midnight school... Ain't I got a right, ain't I got a right, ain't I got a right to the tree of life... Jasmine has a right, Jasmine has a right, Jasmine has a right to the tree of life. . .*

I wonder what time it is... I can't believe it's been almost two weeks since the party... I look like a midget next to Sister Muhsinah. She looks like an African Queen, even in casual clothes... that's why, that's why the universe looks like you!

I reached over and grabbed my cell phone. I'd come home and passed out, just like I did on Monday and Tuesday. Eight thirty. I had three text messages. Dionna and Amber are hanging out in Pura Belpré Park. Dionna and Amber are leaving to go to Dionna's. Derek wants to know if I'm ready for tomorrow.

Thinking about tomorrow made me close my eyes again. I tried to forget what I'd seen, but I couldn't. It was the first day of my summer job at *In Our Own Image Films*, and we were learning how to write a documentary film script. Ms. Gates, the owner of the organization and our boss for the next seven weeks, showed us a short film at the beginning of the day.

In the film little Black boys and little Black girls were shown two dolls, a black doll and a white doll, and they were asked which doll was the nice doll. They kept picking the white doll. Then they were asked which doll they liked the best. They kept pointing to the white doll. Then this one little girl chose the black doll when they asked her which doll looked bad! What I will never forget, though, is the look on her face when she had to pick which doll looked like her. I'd seen that look before. In way too many mirrors – after Halle Berry's face had faded and mine stared back at me.

When Ms. Gates turned on the lights and asked us what the filmmaker was trying to say in her seven minute film, we just sat there. Numb. During the film we'd gasped! And moaned. Me, Dionna, and these girls named Kristen, Imani and Analyse. Derek just shook head. Ms. Gates repeated her question as we continued to scream our silence.

"What was the filmmaker trying to say or what did she say in this film?"

Dionna was the first to speak. "That's messed up. I mean—" she had to stop and let her emotions calm down. "—how they gonna say the black doll is bad and the white doll is the nice doll?"

"It is pretty painful to watch," Ms. Gates answered. "I've seen it several times and it's still painful."

"How old were they?" Derek asked.

"Four and five. And by the way, this was filmed at a day

care center here in Harlem."

Like that was supposed to make us feel better?

"When was it made?"

"Three years ago. In 2005. The filmmaker is Kiri Davis, and she was only sixteen when she made it." Ms. Gates let the room go quiet again.

I took a deep breath in, but it didn't help things any. The air was too heavy.

If you had held a mirror up to Kristen's face, you would've seen mine. We were thinking the same thing too. We needed to find the little kids – we had to find the little kids – who picked the white doll and the ones who said the black doll was bad and tell them they were wrong. "I can't believe they chose the white doll," she said. "I mean, they're just little kids!"

"Not all of them," Ms. Gates reminded us.

"Most did," Derek said.

"Jasmine? Any thoughts?"

I had a lot of thoughts, but nothing to say. I was trying to make sense of what I'd just seen. But the harder I tried, the less sense it all made.

On that first day, when I came home, I locked myself in my room and headed straight for my journal.

Hated and despised for the color of my skin
It ain't about what's without, it's 'bout what's within
But you're to deaf to see and too blind to hear
So take a taste of all these words I'm 'bout ta blast in ya ear

I ripped the page out of my journal, balled it up and threw it in the garbage can next to my desk. I couldn't get that little girl's words out of my head. "Because it's black!" That's what she said when they asked her why the Black doll looked bad. "Because it's black."

I took a long, deep breath in and pushed it out slowly. Then, I placed these words at the top of the page, "*My Black Self.*" Before I could write anything else, my phone rang. It was Derek asking if I wanted to be his partner or whether I'd already decided to work with Dionna. He said he wanted to do a sequel to the film we just saw. He said he couldn't get it out of his head. Neither could I, I told him. He said what if we showed that film to other teenagers and got their reactions.

When we told Ms. Gates our idea, she asked us what would be our purpose in making a short film where we got reactions to the film we'd seen. She told us that we didn't have a fully developed concept yet to make a short documentary, but that she'd be interested in seeing what came of our street interviews anyway. She said doing the interviews might give us a better sense of what we really wanted to say in our film. She made us come up with a list of questions we'd ask people. We'd shown them to her on Tuesday.

Because she's Black! How could she say that?... I wonder what her mother said when she saw it?... If that had been my daughter, I would've cried... I don't know what I would've done, really... I opened my eyes again and sent Dionna a text telling her I'd see her tomorrow at work and that I was anxious about the interviews. She texted back. Then I texted her back*: Not scared rlly, just wondering how it's gonna go.*

Then, I sent Derek a text telling him the same thing. He texted back and said he hoped people would be willing to look at the film. He said if they acted like they didn't want to, we could tell them we'd been out here all day and we just needed one more interview to complete our assignment. He said we could tell everybody that actually.

I rolled out of bed and went into the kitchen to see what mom had fixed for dinner. She'd left a note: *Picked up roasted chicken from Market 116. Gone to a meeting. Back by 10.*

Dalani hadn't gotten home yet either. I fixed myself a plate, took it into my room and ate while listening to my iPod. I pulled out my journal and turned the page to "My Black Self."

My Black Self

Dark... like the night sky under a South Carolina moon
Black like my father and my grandmother too
Dark... and black... and cherished by those who know
Black... and dark... and hated by those who don't
Loved and hated
Angry and sad
I'm tired of all this hatin'
My Black Self

Dark... like chocolate that does a slow dance in your mouth
Black like my great-great-great-grandmother Viola Mae Miles
Hated and abused and enslaved long ago
Loved and cherished and set free long ago
Strong and wise
Angry and sad
How could I ever be ashamed of
Her Black Self

Dark... like ebony wood with chocolate brown seams
Black like the children who haunt me in my dreams
Dark... and black... and beautiful for all to see
Black... and dark... and wounded for all to see
Loved and hated
Confused and sad
Please don't grow up hatin'
Your Black Self

Dark... like the night sky under a South Carolina moon
Black like my father and may grandmother too
Dark... and black... and cute and smart
Black... and dark... and hated and despised
I'm angry and I'm tired

I'm happy and I'm sad
It's time to start loving
My Black Self

I'm cute and I'm smart
I'm happy and I'm sad
I have to start loving
My Black Self

"Dalani?" I called as I heard the front door closing.

"It's me," my mom yelled as I took an earphone out of one ear. She made her way to my room and knocked on the door.

"Come in."

"Are you okay? You were knocked out when I left."

"I thought you wouldn't be home until ten."

"I left early," she said and yawned. "I'm so tired." My mom was starting to get those dark circles under her eyes that make you look old. "I spoke with your grandmother. She's not going to be able to make it up for your initiation ceremony— that reminds me, I have to call Iya Makeba to find out what time we have to meet the seamstress Saturday— it's her church's homecoming that weekend, but I told her we'd video tape the whole thing and send it to your Uncle Elijah, and he'll make sure she sees it. We can send Sister Muhsinah a copy too."

"Okay."

"Are you and Derek ready for tomorrow?"

"Yes." I took out my other earphone and pushed my

iPod to the side. "I have something I been working on." I handed my mom my journal, and I followed her eyes as she read. She got to the end and just sat there staring at the page. Then she looked up and locked eyes with me.

"When did you write this?"

"Monday. After I got home from work. After I saw those kids."

"Come here," she said and extended her arms. I scooted over to the edge of the bed and reached out for my mom. When we embraced, I could feel myself sinking. And floating. My body was sinking, but the inside part of me felt like it was floating, and I could feel her strength. It was like her energy was making me stronger and the warmth from her body was warming me. When we separated, she kissed me on the forehead and smiled.

"It's beautiful," she said as she smoothed down my hair. "You're beautiful." She kissed me again, this time on the cheek. Then, she took a deep breath in. "I saw the film yesterday. I was going to tell you last night but you were asleep. You're right, it is sad."

For a while, neither of us said anything as she turned her gaze back to my journal. "I want you to call your grandmother and read this to her. I'm sure your dad would like to hear it too."

"Okay."

"What time are you doing the interviews tomorrow?"

"We're thinking around two-thirty. Ms. Gates said it's not good to do it during lunch because people won't have time to stop."

"You're going on 125th Street?"

"Yeah, we're gonna start there. Then we might go down Lenox."

"We'll go out to dinner tomorrow night. You can tell me how it went."

"Okay."

"Can you type this up and email it to me so I can print it out and put it in a frame."

I nodded yes. If Mama Roxie were here right now she'd say my smile was so bright it makes the sun look like midnight.

"I'm going to show it to Aunt Angie— unless you want to."

"No. You can."

* * *

The next morning, on my way to work, I rehearsed the questions Derek and I were going to ask everyone we interviewed. "How are you feeling after seeing this? Why do you think fifteen out of twenty-one kids chose the White doll as the doll they liked the best? If you could say anything to the little girl who said the Black doll was bad because she's black, what would you say?"

I was still anxious about the interviews but glad Derek was doing them with me. Ms. Gates would be there too, observing us as we filmed. Derek and I had decided he'd hold the DVD player while I asked questions and held the camera. Depending upon how it went, we said, we might switch off.

The first person we interviewed was a mother in her thirties who had three children. She started commenting on the film even before it ended. "See, that's how they be starting. Five years old and already in love with White girls!" She shook her head and sighed. "That's a damned shame."

I asked her why she thought fifteen out of twenty-one children chose the White doll.

"They brainwashed," she yelled and stared at me.

"So, how would you feel if one of your children said they thought the White doll was the nice doll because she's White?"

"Well," she began, "I'ma be honest with you. Black people can be so hateful sometimes! Am I right, Evelyn?

"Yup!"

"Get on your damned nerves."

Oh wow, I thought as my eyes grew big. I didn't know what to say, really, so I just thanked her for watching the film and for answering our questions.

The next person who agreed to talk to us was a man named Roscoe. When the Black children started choosing the White doll, he winced like he was in pain.

"How are you feeling after watching this," I asked as soon as the credits started rolling.

"What's wrong with these kids?" Don't they like playing with dolls that look like them?"

We're supposed to be asking the questions and you're supposed to answer them, I said to myself. "So how are you feeling after seeing this?" I repeated.

"How am I feeling?"

"Yes."

"How am I feeling?" He looked like he'd just swallowed sour milk. Please just answer the question, I prayed.

"That's a damned shamed," he said and shook his head left to right. "Black kids don't wanna play with a Black doll."

"So why do you think fifteen out of twenty-one kids chose the White doll as the doll they like the best?"

"Well, you know what they say," he began as he flashed a half-smile, "light skin is the right skin."

"You don't think that's wack?" Derek spoke up before I could respond. "Naw brotha, I'm not saying that! I'm saying that's what they say!"

"Who is they?"

"Society, nigga. Society. We got that all up in our heads. Even got the children believing that shit! Excuse me."

"Do you believe it?" I couldn't believe Derek asked him that!

"Well, I ain't gonna lie to you, I have been known to dabble in a little white meat from time to time. Excuse me sister," he said as he turned quickly to me.

I glared at him. It was time for him to leave! Derek just looked at him like he was crazy and stuck out his hand.

"Thank you for your time, sir."

"No problem," he said and paused. "So uh, do I get something for being in y'all's film?"

Oh, I got this, I thought as I waved Derek off. "Thank you very much," I told Roscoe as I cocked my head to the side and put on the most fake smile I could manage. Say something, I screamed inside. Say something!

"It's cool, sister. It's cool."

Ms. Gates walked over rolling her eyes and shaking her head. "So, you're going to get as many different responses as the number of people you interview," she said. "And yes, some will be quite interesting – to say the least."

She was right. By the time we were done, we'd interviewed five people in their thirties and forties, Roscoe, who was in his fifties, one seventy-three-year-old lady and a group of five teenagers. Three were in high school and two were in middle school. I told Ebonee all about what everyone had said while I waited for my mom to get off work and take me to dinner. "He was so disgusting," I said. "I don't even want to think about ROSCOE and his nasty self."

"What about the kids in high school?"

I took a deep breath in before I began recreating what they'd said. "So this one boy said he only dates light-skinned girls. Derek was asking the questions then, and when he asked him why, the boy said, 'it don't fit me.'"

"What don't fit him?"

"Dark-skinned girls. Him being with a dark-skinned girl."

"And how he look?"

"Ugly. I mean, he wasn't all that! Then had the nerve to say he could run down any type."

"Uh huh."

"One boy said he liked all skin colors, and another boy said if you're cute it doesn't matter."

"Was he cute?"

"Yeah. But he's just an eighth-grader. There was one lady who was really cool. She gave us her business card and said to call her when we were done 'cause she wants to see the film."

"What does it say on her card? I mean what does she do?"

"She's a lawyer. Yeah, a lawyer," I said as I pulled out her card. "She started tearing up during the film. She said she had a daughter in college, and she thought things had gotten better for kids today. I told her no. Kids still make fun of dark-skinned girls and say really hurtful things."

"Jazz, I always stick up for you when they be making jokes about dark-skinned girls."

"You do?"

"Yes. I know they be joking around sometimes, but deep down, some of them really think like that."

All this time, I'd been mad at Ebonee because I didn't think she understood what I was going through. I wanted to tell her I used to cry myself to sleep wishing I could be her. I wanted to tell her how good it felt to know she *always* had my back. How good it felt to know she did understand what I'd been going through. I was feeling like the worst friend in the world, though, knowing I'd been completely wrong about her.

"Does it bother you when so many boys like you?"

"Not that they like me. But that they only like me for one thing? Yeah, that bothers me."

"It was like that for my mom. When she was in high school."

"She told you that?"

"Yeah."

"All I know is, next year, if niggas try to feel my butt when we change classes, I'm wilding out. I don't care if I get suspended."

"I have to ask you something."

"What?"

"I been thinking about getting twists, like this girl I saw in South Carolina. Sister Muhsinah's niece. I texted you a picture of us at my grandmother's party."

"Oh yeah, her."

"Do you think they'd look good on me?"

"Yeah, I think they'd look good on you."

"You do?"

"Yeah. But it should be what you think, Jazz," Ebonee said just before she had a sneezing fit.

"Are you okay?"

"Yeah. I'm sorry. The allergies are really bad down here. There's mad yellow stuff all over my uncle's car. They said it was pollen. I didn't know you could see pollen. You should see how red my eyes are."

"We had the same thing in South Carolina. All over my aunt's car."

"Jazz, I know most boys go for girls that are light, but a lot of dark-skinned girls are pretty to me. You weren't with us that day in gym, but Anthony, with his dumb ass, was cutting on Aminata, you know the one from Senegal, saying 'oh you mad black,' and she said, 'Okay. I love my skin. I wanna be blacker,' and kept it moving. You gotta be like her and forget everybody else."

Everything Ebonee was saying was true and I knew it. I was glad we were finally talking about this.

"So when are you getting them?"

"I don't know. I'm still thinking about it."

"You have to video tape it when you're getting it done."

"Video tape it?"

"Yeah, so I can see."

"There's nothing to see. All she does is wash it, blow it out then oil it while she twists it. I sit under the dryer for however long it takes, then she untwists them and stretches them out."

"How does she stretch them out?"

"Just by pulling on them while she's holding the blow dryer. Aunt Angie explained it to me last week then she sent me a video online."

"Where is your initiation ceremony?"

"Weeksville Heritage Center"

"What is it?"

"It's like a museum. We're going next week to learn about it."

"How many girls are there?"

"Seventeen."

"Have you met them yet?"

"Just two of them, when me, my mom and dad went for our interview. All of us are gonna meet next week for the first time. Then we'll meet a couple of more times before the ceremony."

"We're all riding together, right?"

"Yup! My dad's renting a car."

CHAPTER 16

We stood in a circle with our hands joined together on a warm, serene September afternoon. The grass underneath our feet felt like lush green carpet, and the flowers – lilacs my mom told me later – released a sweet fragrance that made me smile.

A white oak tree and several sycamores stood watch over us as we spoke our prayer of thanksgiving. We were about to officially begin our two-year rite of passage – all seventeen of us – African American, Jamaican, Dominican, Haitian and mixed-heritage girls.

I couldn't thank my mom and Ms. Ervin enough for bringing me to *Sisters in Spirit*. Growing up was hard enough, but growing up Black and dark-skinned and with my parents divorced – in this crazy world? Being with a group of girls going through the same things I was going through, and having the space to talk about it, saved me. The things I couldn't say to Ebonee, I was able to say with them, and when we started sharing that first day, and I saw Krystal and Niani gently wiping underneath their eyes to make sure their eye liner was still in place – I knew I wasn't alone.

"I mean, in my high school last year, kids would joke about each other's nigga naps – girls and boys – and yeah, they'd be playing around, but boys don't take it to heart, they just laugh it off. But girls can't do that." Krystal was sixteen and had just started the eleventh grade. The youngest girl in the group was thirteen and the oldest seventeen.

"Yeah, especially if you don't have a perm or extensions. I mean, it's okay for boys not to have good hair, but for us, it's like it's criminal. Like you should be arrested or something." I'd never said anything like that out loud before. I'd written it in my journal and thought about it constantly, and, if I'd had the chance, I would've said it out loud, but now I was hanging out with sixteen other girls who really wanted to talk about things like this. After our first meeting where so many of us spoke out about the pressure we felt to look a certain way and several of us cried, and, all of us, at one point or another, comforted the sister sitting beside them, I knew I'd found a home.

It had been two weeks since we'd last seen each other. Now, on September 12th, 2008, people from all over New York City and a few from New Jersey had come to be a part of our initiation ceremony.

Before we'd gotten to Weeksville, mom and dad had taken a million pictures. A thousand with me and Ebonee, a few hundred with me and Imani, then another thousand with me, Ebonee, Imani and Dionna, and of course a thousand with me, Imani, Aunt Angie, Dalani and mom. Then my dad asked Ebonee to take a picture of him and me together. And do you know that when we got to Weeksville, those fools took out their cameras and started taking more pictures, and the ceremony hadn't even started!

While they were taking pictures, I went away in my head to South Carolina and the week I'd spent with Mama Roxie. The same peace I felt there, I felt here, the second we stepped on the grounds. I halfway expected Grandma's butterfly to come fluttering by and pollinate the flowers. The fact that she couldn't be here but that this place reminded me of her, of watching the sunset with her and working silently in the garden with her as the birds sang and the wind gently cooled our faces, to me, meant she was here.

She would have loved our dresses. We were a sea of lavender waves layered with richly colored purple and white waves streaming across custom tailored cotton fabric and with matching headdresses! We all looked beautiful.

There were at least two-hundred people here to support us, and Ms. Ervin and her husband showed up just as we were about to start, and found a seat not too far from where my mom and dad were sitting.

Iya Makeba and Iya Shawnee walked up front, and the already quiet crowd fell silent. Still. They began by pouring libations to honor the ancestors. Then, they welcomed our family and friends, and they gave thanks for Weeksville. Iya Makeba said it was only right to begin this journey in a place where people with black skin had thrived mightily during a time when black skin was so openly hated and despised. When we visited Weeksville in July, we learned the history of the people who'd once lived there; about how they worked together in their community and fought against slavery and *the idea of white supremacy.*

Iya Shawnee said that in villages in Africa, our ancestors also gathered to honor and nurture their young and prepare them for the journey into adulthood. Aunt Angie later said that as Iya Shawnee spoke, it made her think about her pilgrimage to Ghana ten years earlier. I thought about great-great-great-grandmother Viola, and I wondered if she knew who her parents and grandparents were and what part of Africa they came from.

Then, Iya Shawnee and Iya Makeba introduced the entire SIS team – men and women – and they acknowledged all the elders in the room. There were lots of elders involved with SIS, and every time we met, we began by acknowledging and honoring the elders. As soon as Iya Shawnee stopped speaking, a group of women wearing lapas began chanting – slowly, softly like the rising sun on a brand new beginning-of-Spring morning. The next day, both mom and Aunt Angie remarked that even though we held the ceremony on Saturday afternoon, it felt more like a Sunday. Like church.

Drummers joined the chanters and they performed what we later learned was a welcoming dance called Funga. The dancer we saw in Ms. Ervin's class, Pearl Primus, had learned it from the Vai people in Liberia and she'd made it popular in America.

A ten-year-old girl named Autumn Ptah sang *The*

Greatest Love of All, but if you closed your eyes, you would have sworn she was twenty. As she sang, I watched my father fight a losing battle as he wiped away one tear, then another. The song lyrics reminded me of what Shawnee and Iya Makeba told us about loving ourselves; owing ourselves! During our second meeting, I shared with everyone what Mama Roxie had said about Black people needing a healing after slavery. Iya Makeba said *everybody* needed to heal from slavery!

As Autumn sang, I couldn't help but think about those the little children I'd seen in the video and how messed up that was. When she held on to that last high note, everyone left their seats and gave her a standing ovation.

The minute we sat down, Iya Shawnee told us she needed all the families to stand up again. Each family was asked to state, in front of everyone gathered, their support, not just for their own daughter or niece or granddaughter, but for every girl in the SIS family. Before my dad began reciting the pledge, he put his arm around Dalani and hugged him closer. When he kissed him on the forehead, Dalani lit up like he used to whenever dad hugged him and kissed him.

A few weeks earlier, when he took me out to dinner for my fourteenth birthday, I felt like Dalani did now – like I did when the three of us used to watch basketball games together. Toward the end of dinner, I asked my dad if he knew how much we missed him when he was M.I.A. for almost a year. He reached over, offered me his hand and nodded yes.

I wanted to ask what really happened between him and mom. But since I didn't want to ruin the night, I decided against it. I did ask him if he thought I'd look good with twists. He said I looked good now and that yes, I'd also look good with twists. He said I had to learn to be comfortable with what God had given me, and I had to choose what felt right for me, no matter what other people thought.

Now, seeing him standing there with the rest of my family and friends— that should have made me happy.

It didn't.

I couldn't stop thinking about what everyone shared in SIS – their own stories of being hated on, and how one girl said people always told her she was 'pretty for a dark girl.' And I couldn't stop thinking about what Ebonee had said and what my dad had said...

Yeah, okay, I had to forget about what everybody else thought. And yeah, it *was* stupid to expect other people to love me if I didn't love myself. Still, I wished people would stop saying that! Actually, I had finally stood up to the evil voice inside me, and she seemed to have gone on vacation for the past several weeks. But the memories hadn't. Not memories I could see or hear, but a memory pain that walked with me because it was a part of me, like my heart and my lungs.

My head was starting to spin. One minute I was smiling, just like everybody else, listening to this little ten-year-old OD on *The Greatest Love of All*. The next minute, I was back in fourth grade. With Gavin. And like a drowning person struggling to get above water, the rage inside me fought its way to the surface. I couldn't stop Gavin from knocking me down then, and I couldn't stop him now. I'd returned to that place inside where the memory of him lived. Where there was no greatest love of all. No love period. *But why was he living inside me? Why did he get to be a part of me?*

I wanted to scream. I wanted to bend over, hold my stomach and scream and wail the memory of him out of me. The memory of his hatred for me. For my dark skin. But, as far as I knew, screaming and wailing wasn't part of our ceremony. Still, if I didn't do something, I knew I would erupt into an avalanche of tears. So I stretched my eyes apart as far as I could and hoped no one in my family was watching.

I didn't want to be obvious and start wiping my eyes because then everyone would see me crying. As my bottom lip began to tremble, I tried to force a fake smile while also tightening my face. Maybe they'll think I'm just happy to see them standing up for me. Yeah, that's what they'll think I told myself. *But who stood up for me in fourth grade? Where were you then?*

I cupped my hand over my mouth to try to muffle the pain that wouldn't be held back. I prayed that Iya Makeba and all the families would stay focused on their call-and-response declarations and ignore my meltdown. I closed my eyes and squeezed them tight, knowing that I was going to have to adjust the mascara Ebonee had so meticulously applied earlier that morning. It figures, the first time ever that I wear mascara and I end up looking like a freak show on Halloween. With my head bowed, I rubbed my forehead to make it seem like I had a headache, then I raised my forearm to my head to make it seem like I was wiping away sweat.

Manuela leaned over, put her hand on my shoulder and, in the sweetest voice, asked me if I was okay. She'd heard the desperate whimper that escaped when I could no longer hold my breath. No. I wasn't okay. The pain was too much. It had been with me for a long time, and for a long time, I accepted it. But now, it didn't fit me. I didn't want to ache. And I didn't want to continue to hate. I just wanted to be me.

An elder walked over and repeated Manuela's question. Without moving my forearm, I nodded yes. Then I smiled hoping that would convince her. It didn't. I began fake coughing into both my hands so I could shield my face from everybody and wipe my eyes dry. She put her hand on my shoulder and whispered for me to come. Without looking at anyone, I got up and walked with her, away from the ceremony and around to the other side of the grounds. As soon as I felt like we were far enough away, I broke down.

"It's all right baby," Mama Rosina said as she sat me down and cradled me in her arms. "It's all right."

One side of my head rested heavy on her shoulder as she held the other side with the soft touch of her hand. And as I moaned and mourned and released the memory pain, she rocked me gently. Softly. Then she let me rest.

***

At the end of the ceremony, all seventeen of us stood as they called each of us by name. We were given a journal, a pen, and a bouquet of purple and white carnations as Iya Makeba and Iya Shawnee welcomed us into the *Sisters in Spirit* family. After the ceremony was over, everybody stayed to eat and take pictures of us and offer us words of encouragement and support. Everyone was hugging us and there was so much love pouring out of everybody – like they had way too much inside them, and they couldn't help but let it spill over.

But before we ate, and before everyone showered us with love and hugs and well wishes, before we stood and got our journals and our carnations, and after my breakdown, seventeen men, some in their twenties, others in their thirties, forties and fifties, stood. All of them were dressed in black suits.

They wore black, Iya Shawnee said afterward, to symbol-ize darkness. She said out of the darkness of the womb springs life, and in darkness rests infinite potential. Iya Makeba said that, for the next two years, we were safe inside the *Sisters in Spirit* womb. She said we might not always feel like we understood everything that was going on, but she told us we would always be safe. And at the end of two years, she said, we would all emerge as proud young women ready to embrace the light and stand stronger on our own.

So, the seventeen men who'd been sitting in the front row the whole time stood and turned to face our family and friends. As soon as they stood, two women, starting from opposite ends, placed first a purple towel, then a white wash cloth over the right arm of each man. When the women were done, they took their seats. In unison, the men turned and faced us. I watched as they knelt and pulled out a white porcelain bowl, filled half way with water, from underneath our chairs. Then, each one of them closed their eyes and bowed their heads for a few moments. Afterward, they looked up and spoke directly to us.

Brother Adeyemi, who I'd met when we first came to Weeksville, greeted me by name and told me that he was honored to be in my presence. He put his hand over his heart and said he was proud to share this moment with me and proud to have the opportunity to watch me grow. Then, without warning, he lifted my foot and removed my sandal. My stomach felt a catch, and I looked over and saw all the other men removing all the other girls' sandals.

The water, Brother Adeyemi told me, was scented with lavender oil, a cleansing, healing oil. It was warm, but not too warm, and the feel of it against my skin made me close my eyes for a second. After taking the white cloth and wiping first, the bottom of my foot, then the top, Brother Adeyemi patiently squeezed out the cloth. The soft trickle of water returning to the porcelain bowl sounded like a flute quietly serenading me.

Then Brother Adeyemi took the purple towel, wrapped it around my foot, and with both hands, gently held it in place as waves of warmth and reassurance rippled throughout me. He picked up the white cloth to begin again, and this time, when he lifted my foot, something in me lifted. I felt like Sister Muhsinah walked. Like a queen. And without even meaning to, I slowly took in a breath of fresh air then I let it go.

I had no idea it felt so good to breathe! And if it's okay to breathe, I reasoned, then it's okay to cry – because, like Mama Roxie said, "Jasmine has a right!" So, without trying to hide my tears, and with a real smile this time, I looked out at Ms. Ervin and her husband. Then I looked over at Ebonee and Dionna, then my mom and dad.

And even though we were just starting out, it was finally beginning to make sense.

No matter what had been said and what was done, I'm not cursed. I'm the great-great-great-granddaughter of Viola

Mae Miles. And I'm dark like the night sky under a South Carolina moon. I'm Black, like my father and my grandmother too.

And as I looked at my dad, then at my mom, I saw tears welling up in her eyes, and I made sure she saw them welling up in mine. And in that moment, I knew. I knew that all this time, I'd been wrong too. Just like those little girls who pushed away the black doll, I'd been wrong too.

And even though I didn't know what was going to happen tomorrow or the next day, I knew what was happening now. I was beginning to believe the truth.

I'm not cursed by the sun. I'm blessed by the sun. Rooted in love. And ready to bloom.

***

Author's Note

Weeksville Heritage Center, the site of the *Sisters in Spirit* initiation ceremony, is an actual historical site.

In 1838, James Weeks was no longer enslaved on a Virginia plantation. Instead, he was a longshoreman leading the fight for Black voting rights in Brooklyn New York. Weeks bought property located on the edge of the settled areas of Brooklyn (today Bedford Stuyvesant) from a Black landowner. Even though eleven years had passed since slavery had been abolished in New York State, Black men could not vote or become citizens without owning at least $250 worth of property. Neither Black, White, nor Indigenous women could vote even if they did own land.

James Weeks bought $1,500 worth of land. Together, with a few other free Blacks who also bought property, they established Weeksville. The land was then divided into plots and sold to other Black families, many of whom had come from the South.

Weeksville became a village of free Black laborers, laundresses, doctors (including Susan McKinney-Steward, New York's first Black female doctor), craftsmen, entrepreneurs and professionals. Weeksville's residents established schools, an orphanage, an elderly home, churches, the African Civilization Society, a newspaper, *and* they participated in the abolitionist movement. At its height, Weeksville was home to approximately five- to seven-hundred residents.

It was 1968 when artifacts — illustrated dance cards, well preserved china, glass inkwells, and photographs of well-dressed residents playing cards, sports and music — were first uncovered from the original Weeksville settlement. Many of the original privately owned homes in Weeksville had been torn down by the New York City Housing Authority to make way for public rental housing. But four wooden houses remained.

Not wanting to lose those four houses, the Society for the Preservation of Weeksville and Bedford-Stuyvesant History rallied to have them declared historical landmarks. Members of the Society as well as students from PS 243, activists, historians and archaeologists testified before the New York City Landmarks Commission, and when they testified, they brought with them some of the archaeological evidence they'd discovered. In 1971, the houses were granted landmark status, and in 2005, they were fully restored and opened to the public.

In 2013, Weeksville opened its multimillion dollar educational and cultural arts center.

Acknowledgements

I give blessings and thanks to Janell Walden-Agyeman, manuscript consultant extraordinaire, whose wisdom and expertise helped nurture and shape this work.

Tomorra Hall, Diana Quinones, Janice Ellis, Marcia Thurmond, Taleah Prince, and Susan Wilcox whose eyes, ears and insights were invaluable.

Rita Williams-Garcia for your counsel, mentorship and support.

Cleveland Bennett, for providing me a wonderful space in which to work.

All the students who shared their stories, their pain and their insights with me.

Monica C. Dennis and Shawnee Benton-Gibson, real life rite of passage mentors to so many young women.

Ajzanax, Gabel, Kellie, Simone, Crystal, Brittany, Destiny, Akasha and Shaneil for beautifully affirming this work.

TaRessa Stovall, Vigil Chime and Marcia Davis for your expert guidance, counsel and loving support.

Sister Bisi Ideraabdullah, founder of the Women Color Writers Group, for providing a space for writers to grow.

Bryonn Bain and Levita D. Mondie whose poems, *"Looks Like You"* and *"The Highest Bidder"* so enhance this work.

The People's Institute for Survival and Beyond whose transformative work informs me whenever I sit down to write.

Tewodross Melchishua, my wonderful designer whose spirit blesses me always.

Kristen Willis for being there when I needed you!

Kimberly Collins, writer, sisterfriend, mother, daughter and healer, for your love and support.

Sisterfriends Johane, Mathylde, Shontel, Charmaine and Channa for your love and support.

Lofton Matthew Willis Sr. and Mamie Marie Miles Willis, *always and forever.* Aaron, Janice, Laurie, Matthew and Robert for your love and support.

Deborah Wright, Emily Rousseau, and all the staff at the Avery Research Center for your gracious support and guidance.

The Johns Island Public Library staff who were equally gracious and helpful.

Rev. Joe Darby, Delores B. Jones, Frances Gifford, Bernard E. Powers, Jr., James Campbell, and all the beautiful people in Johns Island for your guidance and kindness. . .

Thank you!

To Purchase Copies of *Like A Tree Without Roots*

Visit Us At

www.atreewithoutroots.wix.com/latwr

Also Visit Us At

www.facebook.com/likeatreewithoutroots

Teresa Ann Willis is the daughter of Lofton and Marie Willis, the granddaughter of Roxie and Lewis Miles and the sister to Aaron, Janice, Laurie, Matthew and Robert. She's a transformative educator who, along with a committed team of parents and teachers, is giving birth to Middle Passage, a private middle-school in Harlem, USA.